"So…what do we do now?" she said into the silence. "Can't we just wait until the fall?"

"No," Sebastian said, slouched low in his seat, arms crossed. "The owner gave me a time limit. After that, the deal's off, and he'll find a 'real' professional. So, no magic books for you, and no money for me."

They relapsed into silence.

"You know…" Sebastian said after a while, "there *is* something we could do."

"Is it legal?" Lily asked suspiciously. She recognized that tone of voice. Sebastian adopted it right before he suggested something wild and dangerous that usually got them into trouble.

"Weeell, depends on how you look at it. We wouldn't be hurting anything, if that's what you mean."

Lily glared. "No, that's *not* what I mean. I mean exactly what I say. Is it legal?"

"No," Sebastian admitted, and there was a pregnant pause.

The seconds stretched into a minute as Lily glared, and Sebastian maintained a carefully casual expression.

"Alright, fine," she finally said. "What is it?"

Also by Lydia Sherrer:

The Lily Singer Adventures Series

Love, Lies, and Hocus Pocus Book 1: *Beginnings*
Love, Lies, and Hocus Pocus Book 2: *Revelations*
Love, Lies, and Hocus Pocus Book 3: *Allies* (coming soon!)
Love, Lies, and Hocus Pocus Book 4: *Legends* (coming soon!)

Hope: A Short Story

The LILY SINGER Adventures Book 1

BEGINNINGS

LYDIA SHERRER

Chenoweth Press

LOVE, LIES, AND HOCUS POCUS
The Lily Singer Adventures Book 1: Beginnings

ISBN 13: 978-0-9973391-0-9 (paperback)
ISBN: 978-0-9973391-1-6 (ebook)

Published by Chenoweth Press 2016

Louisville, KY, USA

Cover art and design by Tony Warne: jedi-art-trick.deviantart.com

Interior illustrations by Serena Thomas

To my family, who never stopped believing in me

Acknowledgments

Many overflowing thanks to the people who made this book happen. There were my faithful beta readers, who never complained about my ridiculous deadlines. Also to "blame" is my good friend Reggie Van Stockum, who first told me I should publish and lent me his copy of Writer's Market (he had no idea the maelstrom he was unleashing upon the world). Then there's my wonderful editor, Lori Brown Patrick, who took a chance with me. Much thanks to my exceptionally skilled and patient cover artist, Tony Warne, and my ever-helpful fellow authors, Robert Turk, Terry Maggert, Jessica Sherwood, and editor Alexandra Birr. I'm also indebted to Joseph Hagan; Maria Bowden and Richard Powell; and Brent, Karen, and Sylvia Hinton, whose generosity helped make this book happen. Most special thanks to my wonderful parents and sisters who have spent hours reading and editing my attempts at writing, never once discouraging me from doing what I love. And lastly, to my beloved husband, who, one cold winter night over a year ago, helped me conceive this story and has been my sounding board, biggest fan, and greatest supporter ever since.

Contents

Episode 1
Hell Hath No Fury

Episode 2
Möbius Strip

Episode 1

Hell Hath No Fury

Chapter 1

Environmentally Friendly Burgers

LILY SINGER WISHED SHE COULD SIMPLY SAY HER DATE WAS GOING badly and leave it at that. But such a gross understatement was against her nature. To be accurate, she would have to admit it was in the top five worst, if not in the top three. This wasn't totally unexpected. Most—actually, all—of her dates were men she'd met online who, inevitably, weren't as cute as their profile pictures suggested. Awkward and bookish, she found it much easier to start virtual, as opposed to real, conversations. Speed dating and blind dates were out of the question due to her abysmal social skills. Well, that, and the fact that she was a wizard.

No, not a witch. A wizard.

"Soo...when you said you had diet restrictions, what you meant was you could only eat burgers?" Lily asked, trying to keep the sarcasm out of her voice. Though she suspected the only way her date would notice sarcasm was if it was dressed up like a cheeseburger.

"Huh?" Jerry Slate, a good hundred pounds larger and ten years older than his profile picture suggested, looked up from his second burger to stare, confused, at her face.

"When we were setting up the date, you asked if you could pick the restaurant because you said you had diet restrictions," Lily reminded him.

"Oh, yeah. I have a sensitive stomach. I can only eat 100% pure beef burgers, and they have to be grass-fed. Free-range, you know? None of that GMO stuff. This place uses the best ingredients out there."

Lily resisted the urge to roll her eyes, consoling herself with the thought that it was better to be taken to a gourmet, environmentally friendly burger restaurant than, heaven forbid, a *normal* burger restaurant.

Looking to the side, she gazed longingly through the restaurant's front windows to the sunlit street, busy with lunchtime traffic. If only she knew how to teleport, she could escape this awkward situation with minimal embarrassment.

"So..." she tried again. "How's your gaming campaign going?"

"Oh, it's fantastic," Jerry enthused past a mouthful of half-chewed but—let's not forget—grass-fed burger. Not slowing his consumption of burger, fries, and a handmade root beer float, he launched into a detailed description of his gaming group's latest campaign against...someone. Lily couldn't remember who.

It was a topic she could safely rely on to keep him talking for a good while, though it bored her almost to tears.

Boredom was preferable, however, to the awkward silence interspersed with chewing sounds she'd suffered through for the first half of their date.

Funny, she'd thought that, in person, Jerry would be more inquisitive. That was before she'd been aware of his burger obsession. As she absentmindedly separated the carrot coins from the rest of her salad and stacked them into a tiny, walled fortress between her and her droning date, she realized he hadn't asked her a single question beyond the perfunctory "How are you?" since they'd met outside some twenty minutes before. From the time they'd entered the restaurant, his entire attention had been devoted to ordering and eating, though he had, at least, disengaged a few brain cells long enough to inform her of the best items on the menu.

Come to think of it, he hadn't been very inquisitive online, either. But Lily was good at asking questions through virtual chat. It was like doing research in a search engine. Type in a question, then browse through the resultant dump of information to find your answer.

When asked a question, especially if said question had anything to do with himself, Jerry was obligingly verbose. He went into great detail, as long as that detail involved the hundred different titles in his grunge rock music collection, or his daring feats in the latest sneak attack against his group's unsuspecting, now-no-longer allies.

It wasn't as if she'd had soaring expectations. She'd just hoped for some intelligent conversation about, oh, say, books. Or history. Or philosophy. Or anything that mattered, really.

Some people improved upon face-to-face acquaintance. Jerry was not one of them. Neither was she, come to think of it. But she, at least, didn't bore anyone with loving descriptions of each book in her expansive personal library unless she knew, for a fact, that the person was a bibliophile.

Hands nervously smoothing down the dark fabric of her pencil skirt, she cast about desperately for an excuse to prematurely end the date. She intended to block Jerry Slate from her dating profile as soon as she got home.

Ignoring the gaming babble coming from the other side of the table, Lily concentrated on the fork she held in her hand as an idea came to her. She whispered the words for a simple heat transference spell, her other hand wrapped around the power-anchor amulet she wore tied to her wrist like a bracelet. Her body heat began to seep into the piece of metal, making it grow warm as she grew cooler. When she judged it was sufficiently hot, she made a startled gesture, dropping it dramatically onto the table as she jerked back in her chair.

"Ouch!" she yelped.

"Huh?" Jerry said, stopping mid-sentence. It seemed to be his favorite word, along with *oh*.

"I wasn't paying attention and tried to pick up my fork. It's very hot. It burned my hand. They must have just washed it in an industrial washer."

Jerry reached forward to touch the fork experimentally, hand stopping short as he felt the heat emanating from the offending utensil.

"Gosh, that *is* hot. Are you okay? You don't look so good." Jerry's brow furrowed in confusion. Not even he was absentminded enough to miss the fact that their silverware had been sitting, quite cool and harmless, for a good fifteen minutes since they'd gotten there.

Lily made a show of feeling her forehead, hoping to redirect his attention. "I feel all clammy. I should probably go home. I could be getting sick. Thanks so much for the food!"

With a touch of guilt, she fled the restaurant, not looking back. If she had, she would have felt better. Jerry's momentarily stunned face quickly smoothed over as he noticed the untouched burger at her place and, not wanting to waste food, began demolishing it as well.

The warm summer air felt good on her face as Lily drove her Honda Civic down Ponce De Leon Avenue, heading back to Agnes Scott College campus. Her soft, chestnut brown hair frizzed in the humidity, despite being pulled back into a severe bun. At least it wasn't whipping around her face and getting stuck in her glasses, as it would've been had she worn it down.

Verdant foliage and colorful flowers crowded around the sidewalks, businesses, and houses lining the street. The abundant plant life was one of the things Lily loved most about Atlanta. It made the place feel less like a big city and more like a well-tended neighborhood. Plus, it reminded her of home in the Alabama backwaters.

Pulling into the college's employee parking lot, Lily gathered her things and headed across campus toward McCain Library. Though originally founded as an elementary school in 1889, Agnes Scott had become a college by the early 1900s. McCain Library, built in 1936, consisted of four main floors, a grand, vault-ceilinged reading hall, and three attached floors dedicated to the stacks. It was a beautiful example of Gothic architecture meeting utilitarian building needs and, along with the other Gothic and Victorian red brick-and-stone buildings around campus, made for a beautiful and relaxing atmosphere.

Though it was Saturday, Lily preferred to take refuge in the library and bury herself in paperwork rather than go home and risk the urge to mope about. The tall ceilings, majestic architecture, and quiet atmosphere would calm her in a way no amount of tea or chocolate could. And, of course, there was the comforting smell of books.

She passed a few groups of girls relaxing or studying on the green—it was a women's college, and non-employee males were discouraged from hanging around campus. On this sunny day, the blue sky and warm grass had lured most students outside to study, so she saw only a few scattered girls working quietly in the library's grand reading hall as she made her way to her office.

Her office was a spacious room on the first floor, with a high ceiling and expansive windows. Tall bookshelves covered most of the other three walls, and a large, mahogany desk dominated the center of the room.

With a sigh, she dropped her purse onto one of the two visitor's chairs—both currently pushed up against her bookshelves as stepladders—and sat down at her desk. The desk's dark wood surface was polished to a shine, and each item on it was arranged neatly. Her computer, pencil holder, and file organizer were placed just so, cleaned spotless, and free of dust. Her shiny, brass nameplate was centered and aligned perfectly parallel to the edge of her desk. It read:

Lillian Singer: Administrative Coordinator/Archives Manager

It was a prestigious position for Lily's relatively young twenty-five years of age. But the fact that the previous archives manager, Madam Barrington, had taken Lily under her wing and personally groomed her for the job had made Lily the obvious choice when Madam Barrington retired a year ago. Beyond the Madam's training and endorsement, however, Lily had been well prepared for the job. With four years of undergraduate work-study in the stacks, not to mention two years as head librarian after graduation, her BA in history and minor in classics were just icing on the cake.

Of course, Lily's love of books, organized nature, and library experience weren't the only reasons behind Madam Barrington's choice. The real reason was she'd needed someone to take over as curator of the "Basement"—a secret archive beneath the McCain Library containing a private collection of occult books on magic, wizardry, and arcane science. Being a wizard herself, Madam Barrington had recognized Lily's innate ability soon after she'd begun her freshman year. The older woman had considered it her duty to keep the then-young and inexperienced girl's insatiable curiosity from getting her killed. Madam Barrington had always been frustratingly vague about exactly *who* owned the books. Her job, and now Lily's, was to care for them, study them, and act as gatekeeper to their knowledge. Only once had Lily seen Madam Barrington allow access, and that was to a very old gentleman who'd arrived late one night and whispered something in the Madam's ear. When Lily had asked how she would know to let someone in, Madam Barrington had simply smiled her mysterious smile and said, "You'll know."

Lily's worries had faded over time, as not a single person had ever appeared requesting access in the year since she'd taken over. Though the Madam was tight-lipped on the subject, Lily got the impression there weren't many wizards left in the world. Of those who did still exist, only a select few knew of the Basement's whereabouts. That was fine with Lily, as the Basement was her own personal heaven. Knowledge was the next best thing to life itself, and knowledge of the unknown and mysterious was something she'd craved ever since she could remember, long before she had found out she was a wizard and started learning the craft under Madam Barrington's tutelage.

That thirst got her into trouble on some occasions. But just as often, it resulted in exciting discoveries which added to her already encyclopedic mind. Having all of Agnes Scott's stacks, archives, and considerable online research capability at her fingertips was a dream come true, not even counting the Basement.

Now, having settled into her leather desk chair in the sunlit office, Lily relished a moment of glowing satisfaction as she surveyed her domain. Taking a deep breath, she let the disappointment and frustration of an abysmal date fade away, refocusing instead on all the good things in life. Books. Tea. Chocolate. Cats. More books. Who cared about men and dating when you had all that at your fingertips?

Speaking of men…

There was a flourishing knock on her office door and, without waiting for an answer, a tall, lanky man with mussed brown hair came swaggering through. His untucked shirt and worn pants gave him a disheveled look, though he walked as if he wore the finest Italian suit in all the world. On a leather cord around his neck hung a triangular stone with a hole in the middle. She'd always wondered what it was but wasn't one to ask personal questions.

His grand entrance was marred slightly by the absence of her visitor chairs in front of her desk, which interrupted his smooth transition from swaggering in to lounging handsomely across one of them. Instead, he had to reverse direction and pull a chair over from a bookshelf before settling his lanky form into it.

Lily hid a smile, trying to look stern instead.

"Sebastian, how many times do I have to tell you, you're not supposed to be wandering around campus. This is a *women's* college, and private property."

"Pish." Sebastian waved a hand unconcernedly. "If you're so worried about it, call security." His eyes were bright with mischief. As if to emphasize his complete lack of concern, he reached into his pocket and drew out that silly coin he was always playing with. He liked to roll it over his knuckles and perform other sleights of hand, knowing it annoyed her when he showed off.

Lily rolled her eyes. She knew that he knew that she wouldn't call security. At least, not until he'd annoyed her to the point of losing her temper, which wasn't often.

"And to what do I owe the pleasure of your visit?" Chin propped in the palm of her hand, Lily raised a skeptical eyebrow in his direction and did her best to ignore the coin. Unlike most men, he picked up on sarcasm like a child picked up candy—every time, and with great glee.

"Oh, you know. Just paying a social visit. It's been *far* too long, don't you think? How's the ol' biddy doing these days?"

Lily's eyes narrowed. Sebastian practically oozed casual nonchalance, which meant he was up to something.

"I'd like to hear you call her that to her face. And your great-aunt is just fine. The last time I visited her, she was enjoying a day in the garden."

"Still kicking, eh?" Sebastian snorted, twirling a bit of his bangs around one finger. "Far be it for the great Madam Barrington to grow old and die like the rest of us."

Lily frowned. "That's quite disrespectful. You know very well that wizards tend to live longer than everyone else. If you're going to insult my mentor, at least have the decency to do it behind my back."

Sebastian laughed, making a dismissive gesture. "Lighten up, Lily. It was just a joke. She *did* disown me, after all. I'd say that at least gives me the right to make jokes about her."

Unlike his great-aunt, Sebastian Blackwell was a witch. No, not a wizard. A witch. The difference came from the source of their power: a wizard's was innate, cultivated through discipline and study, channeled and shaped by will and word, often supplemented by a collection of arcane objects; a witch's was entirely acquired through the delicate art of give and take. Many beings—spirits, demons, and magical creatures—were happy to give aid or favors to the right person in exchange for the right thing. Others could be tricked, a few could be forced, and some were to be avoided altogether.

To drastically oversimplify, wizards were born; witches were made. Though Madam Barrington was always vague when it came to wizard culture, Lily at least knew that not all children of wizards were wizards themselves. It was genetic, like eye or hair color. The stronger the wizard and purer the blood, the better chance of passing on the gene, or whatever it was that enabled wizards to manipulate magic. So, being old, proper, and a traditionalist, Madam Barrington viewed witchcraft as disgraceful and lowly, not to mention dangerous. Only shameless fools with no true ability engaged in such activities. Sebastian's view was, since he couldn't be a wizard, he might as well be something. And anyway, he made a very good witch.

Lily happened to agree with Sebastian but never said so to her mentor. It took adept social skills, a clever nature, charisma, and force of will to live such a life and come out on top. She would make a dreadful witch, as evidenced by how terrible she was at interacting with anyone except the few friends—or annoying acquaintances in the case of Sebastian—with whom she was comfortable. The ease with which Sebastian glided around social situations made her quite jealous. He was everything she wasn't: handsome, confident, popular, and good at whatever he put his mind to, though he rarely put his mind to anything unless absolutely necessary. For, as it turned out, he was also lazy, untidy, and undisciplined. He would have made a terrible wizard.

Putting a note of briskness in her voice—she *did* have paperwork to go through, after all—Lily fixed Sebastian with a stare and asked more firmly, "What do you want, Sebastian? I know you're up to something."

"Well it sounds terrible when you put it like that," he said, grinning.

"Sebastian," she said in a warning tone.

"Okay, okay. I'll get to the point. You're no fun." Sebastian raised his hands in surrender, muttering the last part, disgruntled.

"I have plenty of fun. It's called reading books."

"Uh-huh. Right." Now it was Sebastian's turn to roll his eyes. "Anyway, I need your...consulting services."

"You mean you need my help?" Lily asked sweetly, the start of a smug grin pulling at her lips.

"No, I need you as a consultant, one professional to another." Putting his coin away, he straightened in the chair, smiling and spreading his hands wide in a disarming gesture. It was obviously meant to reassure her, but she was not impressed.

"Really? Professional? Since when are you a 'professional' witch?"

Sebastian adopted an indignant look. "Since a while. Can't you just see it? Sebastian Blackwell: Professional Witch!" he said dramatically, lifting his arm to paint an imaginary sign in the air. "I have business cards and everything." His hand dove into the back pocket of his jeans and produced a rather bent card, which he flipped onto her desk with a flick of his wrist.

"Fascinating," Lily commented, voice fairly dripping with amused sarcasm as she examined the card. The front showed a headshot of Sebastian—handsome without trying, as usual—beside his name and contact details printed in an overly curly font. The back had a stylized monogram in purple and gold.

"And what services do you offer as a 'professional' witch?" she asked, fighting the urge to laugh.

"Oh, casting out evil spirits, contacting loved ones who've passed on, consulting the fates, various potions. You know, the normal stuff superstitious rich people believe in."

"Charlatanry, you mean?" Lily asked, eyebrow raised again.

"Hey! I *can* actually do most of the stuff people ask for. When they want something impossible, like talking to their dead pet parrot or predicting the lottery, I make something up to keep them happy. Ignorance is bliss and all that. No harm done."

Lily gave him a hard stare over her glasses. She hated that saying. Ignorance was one of the least blissful things in the world, in her opinion. She believed that "the truth will make you free," a saying which was carved into the rafters of McCain Library's grand reading hall. But she reminded herself that Sebastian wasn't her problem and got back to the point. "So, what do you need my 'consulting services' for?"

"Well, I got hired for this job, see, and I've run across something more up your alley than mine."

"Is that so?" Her tone remained disinterested. She'd been pulled into too many of his wild schemes not to be hesitant.

Though, to be fair, she'd egged him on in many of those schemes, whenever there was knowledge to be had or a new spell to try. Curiosity often got the better of her, and Sebastian knew it.

"Yes, it is so."

"Explain."

"I was hired to cast out this evil spirit, and it turns out the spirit isn't evil. He's actually a pretty nice guy. The real culprit is a spell put on the house almost a hundred years ago because of some jilted lover. The spirit has stayed behind to warn people away from the house ever since. So, even though he has, technically, been haunting the house, even if I get him to go away, that doesn't fix the problem, and I won't get my money."

"Let me guess: You need me to come figure out what the spell is and get rid of it, right?"

"A very astute conclusion! I'll give you an award later." Sebastian gave her a lazy smile and a wink.

Lily was not amused. "You know, you really shouldn't insult the person you're asking help from," she said, giving him a level stare. "And I still haven't heard any compelling reason why I should help you."

"Ah, yes, well." Sebastian backpedaled a bit. Lily knew his good looks and charming ways usually got him what he needed, so she took delight in giving him as much trouble as possible. A very small part of her liked to watch him squirm. Well, maybe not so small a part. "Besides helpi—I mean consulting for the sake of our professional friendship, there's a collection of occult books in the house, which the owner has agreed to give me as part of the payment. I would, of course, hand them over to you, should you provide the aforementioned consultation…thingy."

Despite her better judgment, Lily's interest was piqued. New books did that to her. She could never resist learning new things. And if these were genuine books on magic, not silly mumbo jumbo written by someone who *thought* they were a wizard, they could be valuable indeed. She was always looking to add to the Basement's collection, not to mention expand her personal library.

Still mulling over the possibility of new books, she caught sight of Sebastian's smug smile. She frowned. It annoyed her to be so predictable, but sometimes it couldn't be helped. Sebastian knew her well enough to guess what was going on in her head. He knew that as soon as he mentioned books, he'd already won.

After a few more moments of silence, just to make him sweat, Lily finally nodded. "Fine, I'll help. And wipe that smug grin off your face, Mr. Blackwell. Those books had better be the real thing, or I'll have a word with your great-aunt about all this 'Professional Witch' nonsense."

Sebastian paled slightly at her threat but covered it with a shrug and a laugh. "As if the old bat could disdain my existence any more than she already does."

"If I were you, I'd be more worried about what *else* she might do besides disdain it. Now, when can we look at this house? I'm not going to shuffle around my work schedule for you."

"Why not now?" Sebastian asked, rising and bowing smoothly, arm outstretched towards the door.

"Hmm…where is it?" Lily asked, considering.

"South, past Fort Benning. It's on the Chattahoochee River, a bit north of Eufaula, Alabama, before the river runs into the reservoir. About a two-and-a-half hour drive. If we leave now, we can spend a few hours poking around the house and have you back home by dinnertime."

Lily glanced at her watch. It was one o'clock. Her failed date with Jerry felt like years ago already, though it had only been an hour. Despite herself, the prospect of an unknown, malignant spell—and new books to explore—was too tempting to delay.

"Alright, let's do it," she said, standing up from her desk and moving to collect her purse. "You'll have to meet me at my apartment first, though. I need to change and get a few supplies." She was still wearing the pretty blue blouse, dark pencil skirt, and high heels she'd donned for her date.

"Sure thing, Lil." Sebastian tipped an imaginary hat and started for the door.

"How many times do I have to tell you—" Lily began, exasperated. But he was already out the door and down the hall. "—don't call me that," she finished in a subdued tone. Sighing, she gathered her things and followed him out, locking her office behind her.

Chapter 2

A Crazy Redhead

THE HOUSE WAS GORGEOUS. SET BACK IN THE WOODS AWAY FROM the road, its long gravel drive was lined by old, gnarled southern live oaks, some drooping with Spanish moss. Beams of sunlight broke through the foliage here and there, making patterns of gold on the cool, green ground.

Sebastian pulled his car up around the gravel circle in front of the house, stopping beside the porch steps and turning off the engine. Lily didn't get out right away, but sat for a moment, taking in the scene and listening to the engine tick quietly as it cooled.

With two stories and a full attic, the house itself was large. An impressively columned portico spanned the front and sides. The columns rose all the way to the roof, while the floor-to-ceiling second-story windows opened out like doors onto a full balcony that ran the circumference of the house. Lily could almost picture young ladies in antebellum dresses standing on that balcony, waving goodbye to their sweethearts as the men were leaving a late-night ball.

She was surprised at how neglected everything looked. The house wasn't falling down by any means, but clearly no one had lived there for years. The paint was faded and chipped in places. Odd bits of wooden railing surrounding the second story porch had broken off or were sagging. The grounds were overgrown and wild; grass grew up through the gravel of the driveway, showing how rarely anyone drove over it. The windows were cloudy with years of dust, and dead leaves dotted the front porch and steps.

To Lily, the neglect added to the house's air of mystery. She couldn't wait to explore. What secrets might be hidden inside?

"Come on, let's take a look," she said, unbuckling her seatbelt and opening the car door.

Sebastian joined her on the overgrown gravel, and they both stared up at the house—Lily with bright-eyed curiosity, Sebastian with a bored expression, as if he'd seen it all before. Which, of course, he had.

They climbed the steps onto the porch, old wood creaking beneath their feet as they approached the front door. Sebastian pulled out a large, ornate key from his pocket.

Lily's eyebrow rose in question.

"The owner gave it to me so I could come and go as needed to cast out the 'evil spirit,'" Sebastian explained, adding air quotes to show his opinion of the man's ignorance. "He hates the place. Wouldn't even come inside to show me around. Just handed me the key and made some excuse about a meeting before he took off."

Lily grinned. "Aw, you poor thing. He didn't stick around for you to show off? What a shame."

Sebastian only harrumphed in reply, turning to unlock the grand front doors while muttering to himself. Lily caught words like "unprofessional" and "serious business transaction" from where she stood behind him.

Double doors unlocked, Sebastian pulled both wide open, letting in air and light to the grand front hall. The sight made Lily catch her breath. A large, open room stretched out before her, the space two stories high, its ceiling and walls encrusted with ornate crown moulding. She entered hesitantly, feeling out of place in all the grandeur, and treading lightly on the dusty but smooth wooden floor. Looking up, she marveled at three crystal chandeliers, also covered in dust, hanging suspended above her. A grand staircase wound up and around the edge of the room, leading to the second story. Doors opened to her left and right, and through them she caught glimpses of parlor furniture covered in old sheets. At the far end of the great hall, another set of doors led to a dining room. A massive table filled the space, surrounded by over a dozen chairs, all draped in dust-covered sheets.

"This place is beautiful," Lily murmured, half to herself, half to Sebastian who stood behind her, hands in his pockets. "Why did they abandon it?"

"Feeling a bit chilly?" Sebastian asked, ignoring her question.

Now that he mentioned it, Lily became aware of a deep chill creeping over her. It wasn't the normal cool of a shaded and well-ventilated summer home. It was the biting chill of a cold, empty house in winter. Her breath fogged the air in front of her and she shivered.

"Is that what I think it is?" she asked.

"That, m'dear, is the resident ghost, Francis Jackson." Sebastian grinned, then called out to no one in particular, "Francis, old boy, come out and say hello to my friend, Lily Singer. Remember, I said I'd bring someone who could fix our little problem?"

The grand hall echoed with his voice, then silence fell. Lily noticed the birdsong and soft rustlings of summer outside now sounded hushed and distant.

A breath of icy air washed over her and she jumped, looking around for its source. There, between her and Sebastian, a gray shape materialized. Though its edges were fuzzy and indistinct, like smoke, the shape was recognizable as a tall, handsome man in a dressing gown. He had a trim mustache and goatee and looked to have been in his mid-thirties when he died.

"Hello, Miss Singer. Welcome to my home," the ghost said, voice as faint and wispy as he was. He gave a flourishing bow, reminding her so much of Sebastian she felt the momentary urge to giggle. Behind his gallantry, however, she could hear a note of deep sadness. She wondered how he'd died.

"A pleasure to meet you, Mr. Jackson," Lily said, standing awkwardly. Should she curtsy? Bow?

The ghost of Francis Jackson waved his hand, dismissing her formality. "Please, call me Francis," he said.

Lily nodded, not sure what else to say. Would it be rude to ask how he'd come to haunt this house? She shivered again, involuntarily.

"Do excuse me, my lady. I forget sometimes how very... chilling my presence can be." Francis did something, and the room got warmer, though still not as warm as it ought to have been.

Lily muttered a thanks, trying not to blush.

Sebastian saved her from the awkward moment by suggesting they all go sit down so Francis could fill her in on the details of their "little problem."

Francis led them to a side parlor, well lit by floor-to-ceiling windows that looked out onto the front and side porches. It was filled with several wingback chairs, various couches, some side tables, and even a piano in the corner. All were draped with dusty sheets, and one chaise lounge already had a Sebastian-sized indent in it. Obviously this wasn't the first time he'd been here chatting with Francis.

The two humans settled onto pieces of furniture. Lily eased gingerly into a wingback, trying to disturb the antique chair as little as possible, while Sebastian flung himself across the already-dented chaise lounge as if he owned it. Lily glared disapprovingly in his direction, but he ignored her.

Francis, too, sat in a wingback chair, though part of his insubstantial body sank beneath the sheet draped across it, so all they could see of him was from the knees down and the chest up. The ghost glanced longingly to one side, at the end table beside his chair. Lily wondered if it had held his pipe or snuff box in years past.

"I was born in the late 1800s and raised in this house," Francis began in his wispy voice. "My father was a wealthy businessman, and he built it for his wife, who came from rich plantation stock and was used to such grandeur. I grew up rather spoiled, I am sorry to say, and in my younger years was quite the ladies' man. My parents threw balls and parties almost every week, and at each one I would woo another girl. But one night, I met a ravishing young lady named Annabelle Witherspoon. She was the picture of fiery passion, with long red curls and luscious lips. I was enamored at once and employed every gentlemanly and romantic gesture to gain her good graces. We fell deeply in love, and I proposed to her soon after. It was rash of me, I know, but I was young and drunk on love.

"Sadly, the naive perfection was not to last. I had proposed heedlessly and ignored many warning signs. Annabelle was witty, quick to laugh, and kind-hearted in her own way, yet exceedingly vague about her family and past. It was only later, after severe disapproval from my parents prompted an investigation into her background, that I discovered the ruin of her family name and the loss of their fortune several years before. In addition, she displayed frightening mood swings, as sweet as a buttercup in spring one moment, then cross and unpleasant as a spoiled child the next.

"I ignored these episodes, passing them off as isolated outbursts, perfectly normal in one as fiery and passionate as she. But when I confronted her about her family, the mood swings increased. Strange things started to happen when she was in one of her moods. Small trinkets flew across the room toward me of their own accord, as if she had thrown them, but not by her own hand. Objects which were not there before appeared underfoot, tripping me. Doors with no keys locked, holding me prisoner to her whims.

"Finally, my parents put their foot down and insisted I break off the engagement. They would let no such unruly, red-headed waif into their household, they declared. I still loved her, but I was nothing without my parents' fortune to fund my lavish lifestyle, and I feared they would cut me off should I stand beside her. I tried to put her away quietly, and asked, rather ashamedly, for the return of the ring I had given her, as it was my grandmother's."

Francis's wispy voice grew even more quiet as he recounted the painful event. "As I had feared, she flew into a rage, calling me ghastly names which, on reflection, I admit

I fully deserved. Yet, having been jilted by her one true love, and with no recourse, she relented, declaring I would regret my faithless cowardice. She began throwing things at me—anything in the room she could lift—and shouted words I did not understand, perhaps from some foreign language, yelling as one crazed that I and my house would be cursed forevermore. Then she fled, sobbing, and I never saw her again.

"Though shaken and ashamed, I diverted my attention to other women and fine wine, eventually finding a respectable girl of good family and fortune to please my parents. We were wed, and my unfortunate past seemed forgotten. But alas, happiness was not to be mine. Slowly, imperceptibly, a pall crept over the house. It drove my parents to depression and sickness. My father was constantly distracted, making poor business decisions and endangering the family fortune. My wife grew cold and distant, and we fought often. An air of misfortune seemed to hang over us. I drowned my sorrows in the bottle, knowing, somehow, that I was to blame, and wondering what Annabelle had done to us. Sometimes, I even wondered if she had been a witch."

Sebastian snorted at that, looking affronted. But Francis didn't seem to notice, just continued his story.

"My wife died in childbirth, along with the baby. I died several years later, alone and in my sleep, of too much drink and a broken heart. They found me, cold and stiff, the next morning. I am not rightly sure how, but part of me stayed behind. I suppose guilt prompted my spirit to remain, held back by unrighted wrongs. I watched from the shadows as my parents died and the house was sold off to cover their debts. The next family fared no better, strife and disaster tearing them apart. The next as well, and so it went over the years. I had no notion of how to prevent these misfortunes from befalling, so I did the only thing I could think of: caused enough mischief to drive the poor fools from the house.

"So here I am today, keeping watch over an empty, cursed abode. My one achievement, not even in life but in death, has been to convince the owners their house is haunted, so no one has lived here for years. I even frighten off the occasional foolhardy boy bent on vandalism. The owners are desperate to sell, but no one will buy. Which is why, of course, they hired young Sebastian to 'cast me out.' But once I explained the situation, he quite agreed my absence would not solve the problem. He was confident, however, that *you* would know how to proceed, and how to lift this dreadful curse."

Francis fell silent, staring intently at her, a flicker of hope on his sad, gray face.

Lily thought for a moment, considering the situation. She felt much pity, both for the mournful Francis, punished a hundredfold for his foolishness, and for the fiery Annabelle, a young girl with a broken heart.

"Annabelle sounds like she was…um…quite a woman," Lily said, trying to offer some sort of comfort to the gloomy ghost.

"Yes," he agreed, sighing, "indeed she was. And yet, hell hath no fury like a woman scorned."

"Tell me about it," Sebastian muttered. "She obviously didn't get the meaning of overkill. That kind of overreaction reminds me of dear Aunt Barrington's choice words when she disowned me for being a witch. Though at least the old biddy didn't curse me. Anyway, *can* you help, Lil?"

Lily turned her head sharply, giving him a pointed glare.

He rolled his eyes, not at all contrite, but giving in for the sake of her cooperation. "Alright, fine. Can you help, *Lily*?"

She pursed her lips, maintaining a severe expression. But Sebastian was unmoved, and she eventually relented, curious about the spell but not wanting to admit it. Apart from Madam Barrington, she'd never gotten to examine another wizard's spells before. She didn't even know any wizards besides her mentor. Focusing on her magic studies had kept her busy since graduation, but this could be the perfect reason to finally start the research she'd always longed to do: searching for her family.

During Lily's childhood, her mother never breathed a word about their family or past, and she got upset whenever Lily tried to ask, something Lily resented. All she knew was that her mother had remarried when Lily was nine. As a child, Lily had always felt different from her stepsiblings but never understood why. The moment she'd turned eighteen, she'd left, sick of the backwater farm life of her childhood, and moved to Atlanta to go to college. It wasn't until she'd been taken in by Madam Barrington that she'd finally found a name to put to her sense of difference: wizard.

Yet even Madam Barrington was tight-lipped on the subject of wizard families, always advising Lily to keep to herself. According to her, no good would come from Lily seeking out her own kind. She claimed it was because wizards were less likely to clash and cause trouble among themselves, and others, if they lived alone, or at most, with a mentor or student. "As troublesome as a house full of wizards" was a common phrase of hers. But to Lily, her past was everything. She wanted to know where she came from, wanted to know her heritage. She felt like her mother had stolen it from her, and she wanted it back. Maybe if she recovered her past, she could figure out what kind of person she was supposed to be. Archive books and Madam Barrington's clinical lessons on magical theory had given her a knowledge only of wizardry, not of wizards themselves. If Annabelle had been a wizard, it was a place to start, a family tree to research.

Lily nodded to Francis, giving him a reassuring smile. "I can take a look to see what kind of spell was cast. Depending on what it is, I may be able to dispel it. But I'm not making any promises. Spells can be as unique as those who cast them, and you often need insight into the caster to undo their work," she said, quoting her mentor. "Counter-spells are much easier; they only need to react to the target spell's effect. Reversing a spell, on the other hand, requires knowledge of how, and why, it was cast."

"Well, that's enough mumbo jumbo to last me a month," Sebastian said, jumping to his feet. "But I assume it all means you have a plan. Where do we start?"

Lily sent Sebastian to the car to fetch her carpetbag in which she carried her supplies. Meanwhile, she talked to Francis, asking questions about the night of his breakup with Annabelle.

When Sebastian returned with her things, Francis floated behind her into the great hall so they could keep talking while she made preparations. First, she laid out a miniature brazier filled with sage and lit it. The herb itself had no magical qualities, but the smell was pleasant and calming. It helped her focus, which was essential for the kind of magic she was about to do. She laid a small cushion on the bare wood floor to sit on, then had Sebastian stand right behind it, warning him sharply to be still and quiet. For once, he didn't joke around. He knew well the dangers of wizardry and wasn't foolish enough to treat it lightly.

Lastly, she took a stick of charcoal and drew a circle around them both. Again, the charcoal was not magical, it merely served as a physical marker to aid her concentration. She could cast a shield circle without it but saw no point in taking risks simply to impress an audience. Risks were for desperate situations. This, in contrast, was research.

Settling down on her cushion, she withdrew a small clay tablet from her bag and laid it on the floor in front of her. It was imbued with runes of power and would serve as an anchor for the shield spell, enabling her to form the magic into a set shape and affix it to something, after which she could release it to do its job while she cast other spells.

Lily took several slow, deep breaths, inhaling the sage. Her fingers curled tightly around the amulet that normally dangled from her wrist. It, also, was marked with runes of power, serving as a focus and amplifier to help her cast more precise and powerful magic. She cleared her mind, then reached inside herself and tapped the Source, the place from which all magic came. Being a wizard meant being born with an innate connection to this power, and the ability to draw on it at will—after much training, of course. For the Source was not sentient, only raw power. And raw power directed without skill or discipline could cause more damage than good. Having power and knowing how to use it were not the same thing, after all.

Magical power drawn from the Source had to be shaped and directed by the caster's will, with the aid of words of power—an ancient language called *Enkinim*, derived from, or perhaps parent to, Sumerian. Passed down over the centuries, the words helped shape a wizard's spells, both activating and limiting their effects. Though many set spells existed, the power of the Source was, in theory, limited only by the willpower and knowledge of the caster. The stronger a wizard's will, the more adroit his mind, and the better his understanding of Enkinim, the more he could do with magic. A wizard could also use *dimmu*, the written form of Enkinim, to make runes, imbuing objects with magic.

Now fully connected—in communion, as it were—with the Source, Lily spoke words of power, visualizing a shield which would block the effects of any spell she might trigger as she probed the curse cast by Annabelle. Magic flowed out of her, following the blueprint in her mind as her will shaped it to form an invisible bubble. This she anchored to the clay tablet, commanding the permanent parameters of the spell as she broke it off from the Source's flow and let it sink into the runes on the tablet. Now the tablet held the shield, and she could turn her mind to other things.

She took several more deep breaths of sage before expanding her awareness over the whole house, searching for signs of magic. She didn't have to look far: it was everywhere. She hadn't noticed it when she'd first entered the house because of how subtle it was, sunk into every board, nail, and stone around her. This was no flashy, instant-effect spell. Its aura was so imperceptible, you'd never notice it unless you knew what to look for. Its effect did not take place in days, or even weeks, but was a slow-moving poison that took months to seep in. The spell appeared in her mind as a dark, viscous mist seeping out of every pore of the house's ancient frame. It was the work of a hundred-year-old curse, oozing sadness, depression, spite, jealousy, despair, madness, and every imaginable thing opposite to happiness and peace.

Lily was awed. What power, force of will, and intuitive creativity Annabelle must have had to create such a long-lasting and complex spell. It had to have an anchor somewhere, a physical object she'd attached the spell to.

Unfortunately, the anchor could be anything; runes could be made on the fly and concealed from the human eye. Though an individual could be protected from the curse's influence by magical shielding, the only way to get rid of it for good would be to destroy the anchor. Even then, such an act would only eliminate the source of this viscous mist. For all she knew, once the anchor was gone, the mist would take years, perhaps decades, to fade. Maybe it never would. She had to find a way to *unmake* the curse. It needed to be reversed, not just broken.

Lily drew back into herself, having found what she was looking for. She spent a few moments just breathing, relaxing her will, resting her mind. Controlling magic took effort and could be fatiguing, depending on the complexity, duration, and power of the spell. Then there was the giddy high that came with using magic. It was a heady feeling, and it took skill to manage it without becoming distracted or filled with foolish, overconfident thoughts. She'd read about wizards who'd stayed in constant contact with the Source. Eventually, it drove them mad, or else some botched spell ended them forever. Only a few exceedingly powerful wizards from ancient legend, figures such as Belshazzar, Jannes, or Nimrod himself, would have been able to bear permanent communion with the Source. Wizards of that caliber hadn't existed for thousands of years. The Source was a power to be tapped in need. Like any stimulant, too much could be a bad thing.

Finally, she stood up, unfolding herself from her position on the pillow. Sebastian looked at her quizzically and Francis hovered, hopeful.

"Find anything?" they asked in unison.

"More than I expected," she replied, bending to extinguish the sage and pack up her brazier. At the same time, she scooped up the clay tablet and pressed it into Sebastian's hand.

"Keep this on you," she said. "It has a five foot radius and will shield you from any harmful effects of the curse while you're in the house. The enchantment will only last a few weeks before it starts to fade, but we should have things well in hand by then."

"Will do," he said, examining the tablet curiously. "What about you, though?"

Lily gave him a mysterious smile. "Really, Sebastian? I'm a wizard. I have my ways."

Sebastian shrugged and put the tablet into his pocket. "So, *kemosabe*, what's our next move?" he asked.

Her smile turned distinctly mischievous as she replied. "We, Mr. Professional Witch, are going to pay a visit to Madam Barrington."

Sebastian groaned.

Chapter 3

Virtuous Thieves

IT WAS NEARING NINE WHEN THEY RETURNED FROM THE JACKSON mansion, so they decided to wait until Monday evening after Lily got off work to go see Madam Barrington.

As they pulled into her driveway and Lily got out, she took a moment to enjoy the sight of her mentor's house in the late afternoon light. It was a beautiful, historic home in the Queen Anne style of architecture, once belonging to a politician of note. Lily had never gotten a firm answer on how, exactly, Madam Barrington had acquired it. She suspected it was part of a trade in favors. Its asymmetrical three-story facade was adorned with beautifully carved wooden eaves and trim. The Dutch gables, wrap-around porch, and square tower on one side all had slate roofs, the gray stone mottled with age.

They climbed the porch steps and Lily rang the doorbell. After a minute with no answer, she rang again, listening carefully as she kept half a mind on her firm grip on Sebastian's upper arm. She probably didn't need it at this point; once she'd dragged him from the car, he'd come along quietly. But she thought he might make a break for it when Madam Barrington answered the door, so she held on, just in case.

"Well, looks like nobody's home," Sebastian said brightly after another minute. "Let's be going, shall we?" He turned to make a hasty retreat, but was pulled up short by Lily's iron grip.

"Oh, stop being such a baby," she said, exasperated. "You're a grown man, for goodness sake. She's your aunt, not an ax murderer."

"I'd rather face an ax murderer," Sebastian muttered, attempting to extricate his arm from Lily's grasp. When she didn't loosen her grip in the slightest, he changed tactics. "Look, Lily, she hates me, and I hate her. We get along best when *not* in each other's presence. Let's let sleeping dogs lie, please?"

"First of all, she does *not* hate you, and I'm sure you don't hate her, either. She is disappointed in your choices, that's all, and you're probably hurt by her rejection. But regardless of your relationship with her, this is *your* adventure I'm helping with, and you *will* man up to it. It will do her good to see you helping people with your skills. Now hush and be patient. It's a big house. She was probably in the garden and it takes time to get to the door."

Indeed, after a few more moments, there came the sound of footsteps, then the clatter of a bolt being drawn back. The door opened to reveal an older woman. She looked every inch the austere matron. Her silver-grey hair was pulled back in a tight bun and she wore a vintage blouse tucked into a long, fitted black skirt. On the whole, she looked distinctly un-wizard-like, except for an exotic antique brooch at her throat, pinned to the high, ruffled collar of her blouse. It was large, oval, and a deep shade of amethyst. It would look normal enough to mundanes—that is, people without magic—but Lily could see the blaze of magic on it and the lines of intricate, powerful dimmu runes around its edge.

Aside from the brooch, Madam Barrington appeared to be a normal woman in her sixties, with high cheekbones and a sharp nose that complemented her well-preserved face and gave her a stately look. Of course, Lily knew she was much older than sixty. How much older, she had no idea, but enough that her mentor's youthful appearance would not have been considered "normal" by mundanes. Something about the use of magic had a rejuvenating effect, which was why wizards aged so well. They still got old and died, but long after their mundane peers.

Upon opening the door, Madam Barrington's blue-grey eyes warmed in welcome for Lily. But then, the door swung fully ajar and she caught sight of Sebastian. Her expression immediately turned sour, eyes cooling to arctic temperatures. Thin lips pursed in a stern expression, she did not move to invite them into the house.

"Ms. B., I apologize for calling so unexpectedly, but Sebastian came to me for consultation on a problem he's helping a friend with," Lily said hastily, putting emphasis on the word *helping*. Madam Barrington's expression did not soften, but neither did she close the door, so Lily continued. "It involves a malignant spell, and I needed a bit of advice on the best way to undo it. I wondered if we might discuss it over tea?"

For a moment, Lily wasn't sure which way it would go. But finally, Madam Barrington gave a tiny sigh and stepped back, motioning them to enter. "Of course, Miss Singer. Do come in," she said stiffly.

She led them down a long hallway to a sunroom at the back of the house. It was tastefully decorated with antique furniture and potted plants. The glass walls and slanted glass ceiling let in the light of the setting sun and overlooked a verdant flower garden. Lily and Sebastian took seats in cushioned chairs as Madam Barrington disappeared through another doorway, coming back several minutes later with a tea tray. Sebastian eyed the tasty spread but didn't move to touch it, which made Lily smile to herself.

She and Madam Barrington engaged in pleasant small talk—a bit stiff on the Madam's part, but still warm. Lily hadn't gotten to visit much during spring semester because of work at the library, so it was good to catch up. Despite her mentor's formal and stiff manner, they had worked closely together for almost seven years now and had developed a comfortable understanding.

After a short while, they heard the whistle of the teapot, and Madam Barrington excused herself to prepare the tea.

"You know," Lily said, regarding Sebastian, "the food is for eating, not decoration." She matched words with action and began to daintily sample the tasty morsels.

"And get another hex? I'll pass, thanks," Sebastian said, sitting on his hands.

"Don't be silly. Ms. B. wouldn't hex food offered to a guest. It just isn't done. Wait, *another* hex?" Lily asked, amused and curious.

"Forget I mentioned it," mumbled Sebastian. He was saved from further questioning when Madam Barrington returned, carrying a large silver teapot.

She and Lily enjoyed their cups of tea in leisurely silence, Madam Barrington pointedly ignoring her great-nephew's presence. Sebastian neither asked for, nor was offered, any tea.

Once their first cup was done, Madam Barrington broke the silence.

"Now, Miss Singer, what is this matter of a malignant spell you mentioned?"

Lily launched into her story, explaining about the ghost of Francis Jackson, his jilted fiancée, Annabelle Witherspoon, and the curse cast upon the house. She left out the details of exactly why Sebastian had begun investigating in the first place, simply implying he was helping a friend. She described, in detail, her examination of the spell, and they discussed it in magical terms, ignoring the glazed look that came over Sebastian's face as things got technical. Lily was surprised by his unusual lack of interruptions and snide comments. It seemed he'd settled on being very still, and very quiet, as the most reliable survival technique to get him out of his great-aunt's house unscathed.

After a lengthy discussion of spell types, casting techniques, and the subtleties of Enkinim, Madam Barrington sat back in her chair, considering.

"Well," she finally said, "it is clear this spell is quite advanced. I have never heard of such vague yet effective parameters. That is not to mention the strength of the casting, to remain active for so long. I have also never heard of an Annabelle Witherspoon in any wizard circle, but then she would have been before my time here in America."

Lily's ears perked at that. The Madam had never offered, nor had Lily ever asked, anything about her past. Now, no longer under the stern woman's direct tutelage, and more sure of her own abilities, she felt bold enough to ask a personal question.

"If I may, Ms. B, weren't you born here?" Her mentor had the faintest of British accents, and it had always made her wonder.

Madam Barrington gave her a level look, as if considering whether to answer such a forward inquiry. After a moment she looked away, gazing out into the garden.

"I was born and raised in Aylesbury, England," she said in a quiet voice. "But that was many, many years ago."

There was a heavy silence, which Lily dared not break. But then Madam Barrington seemed to snap back to the present and continued as if nothing had happened.

"No matter her skill, I would guess Miss Witherspoon came to a bad end after she left Mr. Jackson. If she were as unbalanced as you imply, it would only have been a matter of time before her reckless behavior caught up with her. That, added to her family's disgrace, might have caused enough scandal to get her in the local histories. The only dependable way of dispelling the curse is to find her original notes, if she even kept them. If you find those, the methodology we discussed could unmake the casting. Without them, you run the risk of unpleasant side effects, backfires, and mutations. Unless, of course, you use a blood-binding. But that would be a foolish risk for little gain. No, thorough research is your ally here. I am sure that will pose no problem for you, dear; you did, after all, learn from the best."

Mentor and student shared a private smile. Lily remembered blissful hours lost in the exciting—to her—world of library research. Finding the right book among the sea of volumes at her own library, not to mention libraries and bookstores across the nation, was just as exciting as reading the actual material she sought. There had to be a local library or historical society that carried records on Annabelle Witherspoon. Finding it would be a challenge she was eager to begin.

She thanked her mentor, and, after one more cup of tea, escorted Sebastian through the house and out the front door. Once again, she had to keep a tight grip on his arm, not to drag him forward, but to keep him from bolting for the car at full speed. It would have been an intolerably rude gesture, despite the sardonic smile it surely would have elicited from Madam Barrington.

They relocated to Lily's apartment—and its accompanying high-speed Internet connection—since Sebastian wasn't allowed on campus at the McCain Library, and since his own apartment was a den of discarded pizza boxes and smelly socks. The last time Lily had dared enter, she'd nearly fainted from the overwhelming smell as well as a nearly insane need to scrub the place to within an inch of its life.

Sebastian insisted on sticking around for this research portion of the project, claiming he needed to "supervise" its progress. Lily knew it was his excuse to gain access to the cake-dome in her kitchen—always full of home-made goodies she baked to accompany her tea—and the sinfully comfortable sofa in her living room.

Her cat did not object to the intrusion. This was probably because it assured him vigorous pettings while Lily was absorbed at her computer. Much to her cat's annoyance, her desk was one of the few "no cat" zones in the house, the other being the kitchen counters, since Lily disliked finding cat hairs in her food.

For reasons she didn't quite understand, it irked her that her feline companion, who turned up his whiskered nose at every other stranger, had taken to Sebastian so readily. Right now, he was sitting contentedly on Sebastian's stomach as her "colleague" lay sprawled across her couch, munching on a cheese scone. With white-tipped paws tucked daintily underneath his fluffy gray body, he eyed her lazily across the room as though he, too, were supervising her. White chest markings extended up to frost his nose, and a curious circle of white around one eye made it look like he wore a monocle. As a kitten, these markings had earned him his name, Sir Edgar Allan Kipling, after two of Lily's favorite poets. Now, they made him look particularly scholarly as he observed her with bright yellow eyes.

Lily snorted at the sight and turned back to her desk. The first thing she checked for information about Annabelle was her personal archive. Not her library—that was a collection of mundane books neatly organized on bookshelves all over the house. Because keeping genuine occult books in an insecure location was unsafe—more for the books than for the mundanes who stumbled across them—Lily had a much better solution than worrying about cumbersome protective wards. When Madam Barrington had first apprenticed her, she'd given Lily a wondrous gift: an *eduba*. While the word meant simply "library" to the ancient Sumerians, for wizards it described their personal archives of knowledge, their *grimoires*, so to speak. Yet unlike what mundanes considered to be a book of magic, edubas were full of much more than simply spells. They contained centuries of history, research, and personal notes as they were passed on, usually from parent to child or teacher to student within powerful wizard families.

Of course, all that information had been beyond her reach when she'd first started learning magic. Unlike mundane books, you couldn't just "flip" to the desired page in an eduba. Their knowledge was magically archived, and the information desired had to be called to the physical volume to be read. If you didn't know what to summon, obviously you could not summon it. Madam Barrington had slowly taught her how to access the basic information she needed—spell charts, reference notes, dimmu diagrams, and the like—but she knew there was much more hidden away that she would be discovering for years to come.

The tome itself was larger than a novel but smaller than a textbook. Bound with blood-red leather, its embossed surface was covered in golden filigree tracing exotic patterns that looked faintly Persian. When opened, its thick, creamy pages appeared blank. Only when a wizard who knew the book and its secrets actively called upon its knowledge did text appear on the pages. The glory of an eduba was that it had an unlimited capacity to store knowledge, if you knew the right magic to properly archive and organize it all. In addition to showing her how to retrieve certain parts, Madam Barrington had taught Lily how to create her own entries, thus making the eduba her journal, notebook, and reference book all in one. Though her teacher refused to discuss it, Lily imagined this eduba had been passed down through Madam Barrington's family for generations and she, with no children of her own, had passed it on to Lily.

After a thorough search, however, Lily found no mention of Annabelle or even the Witherspoons in general. Possibly, the Witherspoons simply hadn't been well known. However, her eduba was suspiciously lacking in any wizard genealogies more recent than a thousand years ago—the fault of her mentor's meddling, she assumed—so it was hard to know for sure. Accepting the dead end, Lily turned to that greatest of archives, the Internet. Two hours and five scones later—four and a half of those consumed by Sebastian, the remaining half thoroughly licked by Sir Kipling—she found what she was looking for.

"So," Lily explained, having moved to the floor, where she sat drinking a cup of Twinings Assam tea, "there's a small, local history museum in Eufaula that has an exhibit on the Witherspoon family. It might be nothing, but if any of Annabelle's personal possessions survived, they may be at this museum."

"Excellent," Sebastian said around a mouthful of muffin. He, too, drank a cup of tea—he wasn't a complete heathen, after all, though he put entirely too much sugar in it to be strictly proper. "So, when do we leave?"

"Leave?" Lily asked.

"To go to the museum?"

"They're closed, Sebastian, and it's a three-hour drive."

"Oh, yes, of course. Tomorrow then?"

Lily rolled her eyes. "Unlike some people I know, I have a job. With a schedule. The museum is open from ten to four, Monday through Saturday. We'll go on Saturday."

"But that's so far away!" Sebastian exclaimed, sitting up abruptly. Sir Kipling, startled out of his catnap by the sudden change from horizontal to vertical, leapt off of Sebastian and took refuge underneath Lily's desk, looking affronted.

"What am I going to do until then?" Sebastian asked plaintively.

Lily didn't bother replying to this obviously asinine question, just raised an eyebrow. The "*Really?*" of her expression was insultingly overt.

"Never mind," he grumbled, and got up from the couch to collect his things. "You have no sympathy for the trials I go through, the terrible boredom."

Lily's expression did not soften. "You'll be fine. If you die, I'll bring flowers to your funeral…or maybe muffins. Now, meet me here at nine a.m., sharp, on Saturday. And we're taking my car this time. Last time, I had to ride the whole way sitting on a layer of trash and pizza boxes. And don't get me started on the smell. You should post a biohazard sign on your car door, so people will know what they're getting into when you offer them a ride."

"Yeah, yeah. You think you're so funny," Sebastian said as he dug his keys out from between the cushions of her sofa, then headed for the door. "See you then."

"Make sure you bring money for gas!" Lily called after him as he disappeared out her front door.

The museum was housed in the Shorter Mansion, an imposing house built in 1884, whose purchase in 1965 sparked the formation of the Eufaula Heritage Association and helped launch the preservation movement in Eufaula. At least, that's what the brochure handed out at the front door said.

Sebastian was inclined to rush through the exhibits just to find the one featuring the Witherspoons. Lily, however, made him follow the guided tour through each room, taking delight in both his suffering and in the stories of local lore their tour guide shared.

When they finally reached the Witherspoon room, they held back and let the gaggle of tourists pull ahead, giving them peace and quiet to examine the exhibit. It consisted of a series of panels outlining the history and exploits of the family, along with blown-up pictures of its members. There was also a glass display case containing personal items such as a pipe, heirloom jewelry, an engraved pistol, and…

"A diary!" Lily exclaimed in a stage whisper as she caught sight of it. They both crowded around the glass case, bending down to peer at the bottom shelf where the item's label declared its owner:

Personal diary of Annabelle Witherspoon, last direct descendant of the Witherspoon family.

"Yes!" Sebastian yelled, straightening and punching the air triumphantly.

Startled, Lily shushed him. "Not so loud. Do you want to get us thrown out?"

"Oh, stop being so uptight," he said, grinning. "You'd think you had a pinecone shoved up your—"

"I'll thank you not to finish that sentence," Lily interrupted him. She sniffed and turned away to read the information on the wall, taking a few quick notes on a writing pad she drew from her sizable carpetbag.

"Looks like Annabelle died just a few years after Francis jilted her. It says here she was found in her small apartment, having been dead for several days. It doesn't list a cause of death," Lily finished, looking up at Sebastian. "How sad… she must have isolated herself, or else alienated everyone around her, for no one to notice she was missing."

"I wonder what killed her," Sebastian mused.

Lily gave a shrug. "A spell gone wrong most likely, or else a broken heart. But we'll never really know. It seems that, after her death, her belongings were given to a distant cousin who must have kept them in an attic somewhere for decades. One of the cousin's descendants rediscovered them recently and bequeathed them to this museum."

They both stood for a moment, staring at the glass case and contemplating Annabelle's last days.

"Well, what are we waiting for?" Sebastian finally said. "Let's go ask to see the diary."

"No, I'm sorry, but it's quite out of the question," the museum curator, Mr. Hensley, said, shaking his head.

"Not even if we come in after hours?" Lily pleaded. She shied away from confrontation in social situations, but this was work, so she was all business. "As little as thirty minutes would be sufficient. I'm a certified archivist. I know how to handle fragile documents."

"I'm sorry, Miss Singer, but that diary is on display for an exhibit and can't be moved until the exhibit ends and it goes back to storage. Even then you'll need a signed consent form from the Heritage Association."

Before Lily could come up with another objection, Sebastian sidled into the conversation, putting on his most winning smile. "Look, old chap, surely there wouldn't be any harm in giving us a quick peek right after closing before you lock up the building. It would only take a moment, and we could make it worth your while." He wiggled his eyebrows meaningfully.

Embarrassed, Lily resisted the temptation to hide her face in her hands as Mr. Hensley gave Sebastian a severely disapproving look. Sebastian, on the other hand, seemed impervious to the curator's glare. The look rolled off him like water off a duck's back, and his smile didn't falter.

Attempting to salvage the situation, Lily cut in. "I'm sorry, Mr. Hensley. What my colleague was trying to say is we have a very important, time-sensitive project going on at the moment, and that diary is essential to our research. If there is no way to view it while on display, then when will the exhibit be rotated out?"

"Oh, sometime in the fall, I expect." Mr. Hensley deadpanned.

"Why you—" began Sebastian heatedly.

"Thank you, Mr. Hensley," Lily said loudly, talking over her friend as she drew him away. "Have a nice day!"

Once they were safely outside and headed to her car, Sebastian vented his feelings, wild arm gesticulations accompanying his heated exclamations. “What an unhelpful, stuck-up, self-righteous, obnoxious, unhelpful, little prig!”

“You said *unhelpful* twice,” Lily pointed out absently.

“Because he was! There’s no reason at all why he can’t let us look at it. It’s not like it’s the United States Constitution or anything.”

Lily sighed. “He was just following the rules, I’m sure.”

“Uh-huh, sound familiar?” Sebastian said, crossing his arms.

“Oh, hush.” Lily ignored the rest of his mutterings as they got into the car and closed the doors. But for some reason, she was reluctant to put the key in and start their drive back to Atlanta, empty-handed.

“So…what do we do now?” she said into the silence. “Can’t we just wait until the fall?”

“No,” Sebastian said, slouched low in his seat, arms crossed. “The owner gave me a time limit. After that, the deal’s off, and he’ll find a ‘real’ professional. So, no magic books for you, and no money for me.”

They relapsed into silence.

“You know…” Sebastian said after a while, “there *is* something we could do.”

“Is it legal?” Lily asked suspiciously. She recognized that tone of voice. Sebastian adopted it right before he suggested something wild and dangerous that usually got them into trouble.

“Weeell, depends on how you look at it. We wouldn’t be hurting anything, if that’s what you mean.”

Lily glared. “No, that’s *not* what I mean. I mean exactly what I say. Is it legal?”

"No," Sebastian admitted, and there was a pregnant pause.

The seconds stretched into a minute as Lily glared, and Sebastian maintained a carefully casual expression.

"Alright, fine," she finally said. "What is it?"

"We could sneak in after dark and steal it," Sebastian suggested, studying his nails.

"No! I will not commit a robbery."

"We'd give it back when we were done! How else do you suggest we get ahold of it? Would you rather sit there for hours reading and risk getting caught?"

"No, of course...wait a minute..." Lily's eyes lost focus as she considered a sudden idea. "If I could physically hold the book for about fifteen minutes, I could make a copy."

"Really?" Sebastian was intrigued.

"Yes. It's a relatively straightforward spell, it just requires extended concentration for the duration of the process. I use it sometimes to make copies of fragile documents that can't be safely handled without risking damage."

"So, what's the holdup then?" Sebastian asked, excited once more. "We sneak in, you do your little bit of hocus pocus, and voila! We have a copy of the book. No harm done. Nobody will even know we were there."

"No, no. This is insane," she insisted. "Forget I suggested it. Breaking in is illegal, too. I'm an upstanding citizen. I will *not* break the law!"

"I can't believe I'm breaking the law," Lily whispered, still agonizing over the moral quandary even as she crouched in the shadows of a dumpster behind the Shorter Mansion, Sebastian at her side.

"Oh, get over it already. We aren't doing any harm," came Sebastian's absentminded reply. He was busy scoping out the grounds and building before them, making sure there were no guards or passersby.

It was past midnight, and Lily just wanted to get this over with and get home. She'd swapped her heels for a more sensible pair of chucks—she wisely kept a change of shoes in her car. Unfortunately, she hadn't seen fit to pack a change of clothes, so she still wore the pencil skirt and blouse that were her normal casual wear. She hadn't expected to need an "adventure" outfit for this trip.

"Coast is clear. Come on!" Sebastian rose and ran swiftly, half bent over, across the parking lot and lawn between them and the mansion. Caught off guard, Lily scrambled to catch up, puffing slightly as she joined him by the back door. He'd already gotten busy examining the lock, pulling some slender picks from his pocket.

"You can pick locks?" Lily hissed. "No wonder your aunt disapproves of your skills."

"Hey, don't hate," Sebastian said. "When you're a witch, and you have to deal with a bunch of finicky, cantankerous critters, you generally look for ways to do the little stuff on your own. We don't have the luxury of waving our hands and making things just do what we want with no price paid."

"Excuse me? No price paid? It's called we spend decades studying, and every time we tap the Source we're taking our lives into our own hands."

"Whatever. You guys still have it good," Sebastian said, then, "aha!"

With a click of tumblers, Sebastian turned his picks and pushed on the door. It didn't budge.

"Hmm…we may need your Source after all, Lil."

"Don't call me—" Lily began through gritted teeth.

"Yeah, yeah. I know. Looks like there's an old-fashioned latch that can only be accessed from the inside. I could probably bust through it, but I don't want to damage their door."

Lily sighed. "Let me take a look."

It took some fiddling, but she finally found a spell that would work. With a scrape of metal on wood, the latch lifted and Sebastian was able to open the door.

"Wait!" Lily whispered. "What about alarms?"

"There aren't any. I checked things out when we were here earlier."

"Checked things out?" Suddenly, the realization hit her. "You were planning on doing this all along, weren't you?" she accused him as they crept carefully toward the stairs.

"Well, not really. I didn't know if we would need to or not. But I like being prepared, just in case." He turned and winked at her in the near darkness.

"I'm going to kill you," she grumbled, mounting the carpeted stairs behind him. "As soon as we get out of here, I'm going to kill you."

With some difficulty—it was a large house and the rooms formed a virtual maze in the darkness—they found their way back to the Witherspoon room. Sebastian made quick work of the lock on the glass case, and Lily gently withdrew the diary. Settling down cross-legged on the floor, she rested the diary on one knee, then drew out a blank, leather-bound book of approximately the same size from her carpetbag. Next, she got out a bottle of ink and unstoppered it, putting it on the floor in front of her. One of the reasons she bothered lugging the bag around was to have certain essential supplies on hand in case of an emergency, and she was glad she did.

The spell of text transference was one of her favorite spells, and one she was quite good at. All it required was peace and quiet, concentration, and a little time. You didn't even need light, as the magic did all the copying. Hand-written documents were a bit trickier, since you had to use a different variation of words to get the parameters right, but she had experience in both. She was the curator of an archive of spell books, after all, some of which dated back a thousand years or more, long before printing presses.

Settling the blank volume on her opposite knee, she laid a hand on each book and took several deep breaths, settling herself. She let the Source well up and flow from her, streaming from one book to another, taking the memory of words with it. It copied the patterns of ink from stained, worn pages to crisp, new ones. The level of ink in her bottle slowly sank as it was used by the spell. Sebastian fidgeted impatiently from time to time, but Lily ignored him, keeping her full attention on guiding the spell. Losing concentration would create errors in the text, and that would make all their efforts useless.

Finally finished, Lily placed her new copy of Annabelle's diary in her carpetbag and got up stiffly to return the original to its place. They made their way as swiftly as possible back through the mansion, down the stairs, and out the back door. If it had been up to Lily, they would have run off then and there, but Sebastian reminded her that they had to re-lock the door, so no one would know there had been a break-in. Just as they finished, but before they had a chance to disappear, a sudden sound of footsteps echoed from around the side of the mansion, and a flashlight beam could be seen sweeping back and forth. Someone was coming toward them.

Without warning, Sebastian pushed Lily back against the wall of the building and kissed her full on the mouth, just as the flashlight beam rounded the corner and illuminated them. Lily dropped her carpetbag in shock and just stood there like an idiot as Sebastian deepened the kiss, wrapping his arms around her and making exaggerated moaning noises into her lips.

"Hey! What are y'all doing here?" A stern voice called out from behind the blinding flashlight beam.

At the sound of the voice, Sebastian broke his suction hold of her lips and started up in feigned surprise. "Oh! Sorry, we were just…uh…" he did an excellent impression of a flustered teenager, embarrassed to be caught in the middle of his first kiss with a pretty girl.

"You two shouldn't be hanging around here. This is private property."

"Okay, okay. We didn't mean any harm, mister. Just trying to get a moment alone, you know?"

"Well, go find somewhere else to be alone. This is private property," the faceless voice repeated.

"Already on our way. Have a nice night!" Sebastian raised a hand, palm outward in a placating gesture, the other grabbing Lily's arm and pulling her with him as he made his escape toward the parking lot. She barely had the wits to grab her carpetbag as he towed her away.

Heart racing, breath coming in quick gasps—more from adrenalin than exertion—Lily trotted awkwardly, legs restrained by her pencil skirt, trying to keep up with Sebastian's long strides. They crossed the parking lot and turned down the street beyond, heading to where they'd parked Lily's car.

Once they were out of sight, and earshot, of the man with the flashlight, Sebastian let loose his suppressed guffaws of laughter. He clutched at a nearby lamppost to stay upright as Lily walked past, pointedly ignoring him.

"Ah, the old kissing trick," he said, wiping tears of laughter from his eyes, "it works every time. You should've seen the look on your face. And that guy swallowed it, hook, line, and si— "

He was cut off, mid-sentence, as Lily spun on her heel and slapped him full in the face.

"How dare you! How dare you kiss me!" she said, hotly. "I did not give you permission to do that. It was extremely rude, not to mention disgusting!"

Now that she'd gotten over her initial shock, and fear of possibly being caught, she was furious.

Blinking and rubbing his jaw, Sebastian tried to brush her off. "Ha! Disgusting? I bet you enjoyed every second of it."

"I—most—certainly—did—not," she said indignantly, quite angry without exactly knowing why. She couldn't decide who made her more upset—Sebastian for kissing her, or herself for doubting her own declaration of disgust.

Sensing the gathering thunderclouds, Sebastian's grin faded. "Hey, sorry, Lily. I didn't mean any harm. I was only trying to get us out of a tight spot. If it upset you that much, I promise I won't kiss you again without asking first, how's that?" His grin was back, and he winked at her.

Despite herself, Lily couldn't help but smile a bit in return. She suppressed it right away, of course, covering it with a stern glare as she poked him in the chest.

"You had *better* be sorry. Don't ever—do—that—again." With each word, she prodded him harder, emphasizing her point.

"Okay, okay," Sebastian said, raising his hands in surrender. "I get it, you hate being kissed. So noted. Now, can we get out of here, please?"

"Yes, let's," she said, suddenly weary beyond belief. "But you're driving."

Chapter 4

Ga-arhus-a Ken

Usually, once she got her hands on a new book, Lily became oblivious to everything else until she'd read it front to back. But this time, she'd had enough excitement for one night. Once home, she stayed awake only long enough to check on Sir Kipling before collapsing into bed. Thus, it was Sunday afternoon, after a light repast of PB&J and Irish Breakfast tea, before she finally sat down at her desk and cracked open the copy of Annabelle Witherspoon's diary.

A cursory reading confirmed what she'd suspected: the true text was concealed by magic. To a mundane's eye, the diary was full of insipid entries describing the boring life of a privileged lady who spent her time buying dresses and complaining about how dull everyone was. Fortunately for

Lily, she'd used a few modifications for her spell of transference. Several years ago, after trying to copy text disguised by a basic masking spell from a seventeenth-century personal journal, she'd worked out a way to copy both versions of text intact—the real text as well as the mask. All she had to do was figure out what mask Annabelle had used and how to remove it.

As was her custom when performing experimental magic, she cast a circle of containment on her living room floor from which to work. The opposite of a shield spell, this spell kept magic in, lest anything get out of hand. Sir Kipling, the tip of his tail twitching with interest, sat just outside the boundary and watched as she spent the next hour fiddling with the diary.

Having gotten nowhere, Lily threw up her hands in disgust and lowered the circle to go brew more tea. When she returned, she found Sir Kipling sprawled across the open diary as if he owned it.

"Really, Sir?" she chided, rolling her eyes and bending to pick him up and deposit him on the sofa. "I don't need cat hair littering my workspace and corrupting my spells."

She blew hard on the diary, scattering her cat's "gift" of hair, then raised the containment circle again. For a while, she just sat and stared blankly at the book, out of ideas.

Sir Kipling meowed loudly, startling her from her reverie. He was back, sitting just outside her circle and staring at her lazily.

"You're no help," she muttered, then stopped. Maybe he was. An idea had formed, sparked by the vision of cat hair littering the book. She thought for a moment, considering what words would be needed to improvise such a spell.

Once she was ready, she picked up the diary and "blew" across it again, not with her breath, but with magic. As she blew harder, bits of ink, infused with magic, peeled up and flew off the pages, dissipating into tiny puffs of black as they hit her containment circle. With the inane scrawl of Annabelle's "fake" writing gone, a much tidier, neater script appeared. Lily's heartbeat quickened as she recognized Enkinim conjugations and spell formulae crammed into the margins around what seemed to be a dissertation on spell theory.

It took several minutes, but finally all the masking text had been removed, and Lily held in her hands a true wizard's diary. Excited, she dispelled her circle and moved to the desk. With her eduba at hand, she began to read and take notes.

Lily straightened from her hunched position at her desk and groaned. The ornate hands of the Gothic clock on her bookshelf indicated it was past two a.m. She would regret this in the morning, but just now her mind was too full of exciting information to be worried about a little thing like sleep.

Annabelle Witherspoon hadn't just been a wizard; she'd been a prodigy, a genius. It was clear from her notes that she had a deep, almost intuitive understanding of Enkinim and how it was used to shape the Source. Lily had filled her eduba with notes on the diary, sometimes transferring whole pages straight into her magical archive. Her notes allowed her to highlight and cross-reference throughout the disjointed but brilliantly written text.

Annabelle had written more than the curse that plagued Francis Jackson. She'd also written scores of other spells, some of which looked decidedly dangerous. A streak of recklessness was evident throughout the girl's meticulous notes, though perhaps it only appeared reckless to Lily. Despite her youth, Annabelle clearly knew what she was doing. Lily wondered who her teacher had been. He was referenced vaguely a few times at the beginning, but never by name. Apparently, Annabelle's parents had provided for her tutoring up until a certain age, but then stopped. According to the diary, it was because they thought magic was too dangerous. Since that was why Lily assumed her own mother had hidden her heritage from her, it was a familiar point of view. Though, if she'd had a child as precocious, and reckless, as Annabelle, she might have been more sympathetic. Annabelle, obviously, hadn't agreed with her parents, and had kept practicing magic on her own.

She'd kept the diary from 1905 to 1911, about ages sixteen to twenty-two. Except for a few entries near the beginning, Annabelle rarely mentioned her life or anyone in it. Not a word was written about her family's troubles or financial ruin. Instead, she focused on her study of magic. That is, until 1909—the year she met, fell in love with, and was jilted by Francis. During 1909, there were frequent, dreamy entries about her sweetheart. After 1909, however, her writing dropped off to almost nothing. There were barely fifteen incredibly sparse entries over the last two years of her life, 1909 to 1911, based on Lily's notes from the exhibit at the museum. Never once was Francis mentioned by name after 1909.

Lily couldn't imagine how heartbroken Annabelle must have been when Francis jilted her. Just before the point where her entries dropped off, she'd written:

> *August 19, 1909*
>
> *Francis is such a dear, but he has seemed downcast recently. He does not laugh as he used to and has an exceedingly odd look on his face when he thinks I am*

not watching. I do hope my moods are not troubling him. He has always laughed them off before. I do not know what I would do without him. He is the only person in the world who has never held them against me. Not even mama and papa accept me the way he does.

The shock and suddenness of his rejection must have hit so hard she wasn't thinking straight when she'd cast the fated curse. Annabelle herself admitted in her diary when she'd written the spell that its effects were uncertain and untested.

Though the theory behind the curse was meticulously documented, somehow Lily felt it wouldn't be enough for her to unmake it. She could formulate a reversal based on the original wording, but that was assuming Annabelle had cast the curse exactly as she'd outlined it. Lily doubted that was the case. Something had gone wrong. Based on Annabelle's notes, the curse should have only lasted several years, so she must have added or changed something last minute, and consequently it went wrong. Or worse, it went *too* right. Lily suspected it was that "something" which had contributed to the poor girl's early death. Several cryptic entries near the end of her diary supported this theory:

February 11, 1911

Something is not right. Despite my efforts to release it, the spell is not dissipating. There is still a connection, one I cannot fathom. I am sure I made no error. My wording was very precise, perhaps too precise. "Ga-ar-hus-a." *Yet, I already have, so why does it remain? If only I could retrieve the anchor. But I cannot face him. Never again. It would destroy me.*

April 14, 1911

I am so tired. Always tired. What drains me so? I fear I put too much of myself into my revenge. It is sapping my strength. I cannot seem to remember the words the way I used to. Thank the heavens for my notes.

September 2, 1911

It is no use. I am weary with the effort and the burden of it. I want to forgive, to forget. I want it to end. I have forgiven, I am sure of it. But no matter what I do it will not be banished. I know not why, nor have I the strength to care any longer. Perhaps I deserve this unending torment.

That was one of the last entries, the other few being jumbled scrawls of Enkinim and formulae. The scribbles were so unlike Annabelle's previously meticulous writing that Lily assumed whatever had plagued her spirit had addled her wits as well.

Despite the hours spent poring over every scrap of material referencing the curse, she was no closer to discerning how Annabelle had deviated from her own formula. If only she'd said *what* the anchor had been, the battle would be half over. That was the key.

But she hadn't.

A jaw-splitting yawn interrupted her concentration, and Lily suddenly realized how tired she was. She hated going to sleep with a puzzle left unsolved, but her body would brook no protests. Now armed with a solid understanding of the curse, perhaps she could dig up more detail about the casting from Francis. If he could remember, that is. Succumbing to her body's demands, she dragged herself to her bedroom and under the covers. She fell asleep with visions of spell pages cluttering her mind, each one impossible to read because of the giant, key-shaped piece missing from their middle.

The week passed slowly, with many of Lily's colleagues stopping her in the hallways to ask if she were alright, she seemed so distracted. More so than usual, that is. Lily assured them she was fine, and tried not to accidentally set anything on fire as she went about her daily duties, most of her mind preoccupied by Annabelle's curse. She spent her evenings going over the formula, memorizing it and making a list of words for every possible anchor she could think of.

Saturday finally came around again, and she was already up and dressed when her phone rang at ten o'clock. The jaunty beat of the 1960s theme song from *Bewitched* told her it was Sebastian, prompting the usual ironic grin that came every time she heard it. She'd flatly forbidden him from disturbing her during the week, so this was his version of a "crack-of-dawn, lets-get-to-it" wake-up call—to Sebastian, ten in the morning was the crack of dawn.

Lily picked up her phone.

"I'm dressed and ready to go," she said. "I'll meet you at your house in fifteen. Will you be ready by then?"

"Errr…" was his reply. "If I have to take a shower it'll be more like thirty. But if you're in a rush I could skip that part."

"Make it thirty," Lily said, firmly. "I'll bring breakfast."

"Breakfast as in your homemade muffins?" Sebastian asked, his tone painting a vivid picture of puppy-eyed pleading.

Lily rolled her eyes. "I suppose it could be arranged."

"All right! See you then," he said, and hung up.

Lily glared half-heartedly at her phone, trying to feel offended. It was hard to be upset at being taken for granted when it was done with such fawning enthusiasm.

They munched on muffins and bagels with cheese during the drive south, arriving at the Jackson Mansion a little before one o'clock.

While Lily got her things out of the car, Sebastian unlocked the front doors and went inside to find Francis. By the time Lily made it up the steps, the ghost was waiting for her, looking as hopeful and expectant as one could when made of gloomy, grey mist.

"Have you done it?" Francis asked anxiously. "Have you found a solution? A counter-curse?"

Lily had to hide a smile. "No, not a counter-curse. We're trying to un-make it, remember? Not counter it."

"Ah...yes, of course. I must confess I do not quite fathom the difference—"

"You and me both pal, you and me both," Sebastian cut in from where he leaned against the doorframe.

Francis shot him a disapproving look, but continued "—however, I trust your expertise."

"Thank you, Francis." Lily said, bending to set her carpetbag in the middle of the grand hall floor. Light spilled in from the open front doors and lit up the hall with summer sun, making the ghost barely visible where he floated, half in, half out of the sun's rays.

Straightening back up, Lily turned to fix the half of Francis she could see with a serious look. "I appreciate your confidence, but I haven't solved the whole thing yet. There are some critical pieces missing that I hope you can fill in."

"Of course," Francis said, coming closer and out of the beams of sunlight. "Any way I can be of help."

"Alright." Lily got out her eduba, summoning her notes on Annabelle's diary to its pages and readying a pencil. "I know we've already talked about...that night. But I need you to try very hard to remember more detail. Those foreign-sounding words you heard? I need to know what they were and what she was doing when she spoke them. Can you do that?"

"I...." His voice faltered, and he struggled to regain his composure. "It was so long ago...and I am loath to remember. Annabelle was the most beautiful, wonderful thing that ever happened to me. I am eternally ashamed of the selfish attitude of self-preservation that took hold of me. Yes, she had her troubles. But she was a lonely soul, hungry for understanding, and I could have given it to her. Instead, I was too afraid of losing the riches and station I was accustomed to. I acted in a most reprehensible and cowardly fashion. The shame haunts me every day. Worst of all, I never had the chance to ask forgiveness and make things right. My sweet Annabelle went to her grave thinking I did not care. To spend eternity knowing you are unforgiven is pure torment. Yet, if reliving my sins has any hope of freeing me from this curse, I will try."

He began a halting, blow-by-blow account of his rejection, obviously reluctant even now to repeat the excuses and platitudes he'd spoken in an attempt to justify his decision. If a ghost could have blushed in shame, he would have done it.

"...and then she began to throw various objects: books, my snuff box, a vase off the mantelpiece—mother's favorite, she never forgave me for that—and even the end table. She turned over the chairs and screamed names at me, accused me of leading her on and being a coward, a farce, a...well many other unpleasant things besides." The ghost looked down and fell silent.

"And then?" Lily prompted. "When did she start speaking a foreign language?"

"Well, I had taken refuge behind the open door to the next room and was trying to talk sense into her. When there was nothing left to throw she simply stood there and screamed, describing all the horrid things that ought to happen to me. They were quite disturbing. I, ah, politely insisted she return the ring and leave at once, before she did something rash.

"That set her off again, and she began throwing broken pieces of objects she had already thrown. That was also when she started saying odd things. I am truly sorry, but I cannot remember what they were, I have no mind for languages. In the middle of it all, I heard a metallic clink as something bounced off the door and fell to the ground. She yelled a bit more in that language, then stormed out. When I dared reenter the room, I found my grandmother's ring lying upon the floor. That is…what happened," He finished, lamely.

"Hmm…." Lily mused, thinking hard. "Did you notice anything different about the ring?"

Francis thought for a moment. "Not exactly. It looked as it ever had, though it was rather hot when I picked it up."

"Ah ha!" Lily exclaimed. "That's it! I should've known. Why didn't you mention it before? You never said she threw the ring at you."

"Well, I was not eager to remember the…sad details," Francis murmured, eyes downcast.

Lily opened her mouth to reply, but a thought struck her, and her heart sank.

"I don't suppose you still have the ring, do you?" she asked, unhopeful. Such a valuable item would surely have been sold off to pay debts.

"As a matter of fact, I do." Francis smiled for the first time since Lily had met him. It was a small, weak smile, but a smile nonetheless. "After my wife died I could not bear to part with it. I put it in our family safe and it has stayed there ever since."

Lily's excitement returned, though she was skeptical. "But wouldn't the new owners have sold it off or put it in a safe deposit box or something?"

"One would suppose. However, I died rather suddenly, as did both my parents, and the records of the combination were lost. It has stayed locked since my death."

"But why didn't they force it open? Or move it?"

Francis raised an eyebrow. "My dear, that thing is a Hall's Patent safe. Its walls are eight inches of solid cast iron, and it weighs almost half a ton. It was put in place when the house was built, and would take herculean effort to move. Besides, it is a valuable antique and it would not do to harm it. Various owners have considered moving it but never gotten around to doing so. It has become a part of the scenery, tucked away in the upstairs office all these years."

"Well then, why didn't you tell anyone the combination?" Lily asked.

Francis shrugged. "I am a ghost. No one listens to a ghost."

Lily shook her head, incredulous, but grateful. "Well, will you tell *us* the combination so we can banish this curse once and for all?"

"Certainly," Francis said, and gestured with an arm toward the grand staircase. "After you, Miss Singer."

Lily sat cross-legged on her pillow—her preferred position for complex spell-work—and centered herself. The calming scent of burning sage from her small brazier filled the room. There was no shield spell this time: a barrier would create interference between the anchor and the invisible mist sunk into the walls around her. For protection, she had to rely on her personal ward, a much more complex and powerful version of the shield spell. It was anchored to the engraved beads woven into the cord of her amulet bracelet. Its magical power followed the curves of her body, fitting over her like a second skin, quite invisible to mundanes, and even to wizards unless they were looking. Madam Barrington had given it to her when she'd started teaching Lily magic. She'd said it was to "keep you in one piece until you learn some sense." Lily had since become adept at making her own wards but kept her mentor's gift, anyway.

Sebastian watched from a safe distance, observing through the open front door as he stood by her carpetbag containing her eduba and other materials she'd brought. She noticed he was fidgeting distractedly with his coin, apparently unable to be completely still. Francis, however, hovered across from Lily, regarding the proceedings intently. Between them, on the smooth wood floor, lay the ring. Despite its age, the gold band and diamond gemstone sparkled in the sunlight. To Lily's eyes, they weren't the only things that glimmered. She could see dimmu runes sunk into the ring's surface, and they glittered darkly—an impossible feat, yet that was the only way to describe how sharp and *there* the darkness was.

Though aware of Sebastian's curiously impatient stare on her back, and Francis's painfully hopeful gaze on her front, she breathed deeply, relaxed, and took her time, running over the words she would need in her head. When she felt ready, she opened herself to the Source, drawing steadily but not releasing its power, letting it slowly grow in her until she was full to the crown. The ring pulsed with an insentient malevolence, and Lily knew its power, fueled by rage and grief, would not be easily overcome. Steeling herself, she reached down and picked up the ring, holding it firmly between forefinger and thumb of both hands as she closed her eyes and spoke the words of power, commanding its curse to be unmade.

What happened next was like nothing she'd ever experienced or even read about. She knew instinctively as the words left her mouth that her spell was correct. Yet despite her impeccable Enkinim, her words didn't unmake the curse. Her power hung in the air, full of purpose, yet opposed. Something pushed back, as if the ring itself were alive and casting its own counter-spell. But that was impossible. It was inanimate. Even if counter-spells were present, they would have been activated and done their job without delay. They wouldn't have hung there, pushing back with equal strength as though opposing her will.

Straining to maintain her spell, knowing she had to find a way around this or else give up, she probed deeper, opening her mind to the opposing magic, trying to understand it. Deeper she went, until, in her mind's eye, she could see the black mass of clinging mist at its heart. She hesitated. Thoughts of "stupid" and "rash" flashed across her mind. But she'd come too far to back down now. She had to figure this thing out.

Taking a deep breath, she reached out with her mind and touched the mist. It enveloped her, and everything went black.

When she regained awareness, she knew at once something wasn't right. She no longer wore the jeans and t-shirt she'd put on that morning. Instead, she was clothed in flowing black robes. Her senses felt dulled, her body sluggish. The Jackson Mansion was gone and all she could see around her was dark, glowing mist. She turned her insubstantial body, looking around, and jumped in surprise.

Behind her stood a stunningly beautiful woman whose fiery red hair flowed down her shoulders in luxurious, cascading curls. She had brilliant green eyes, strong cheekbones, and a dainty nose. Her heart-shaped face tapered to a sharp chin that nonetheless flowed gracefully into a slender neck. The woman wore a breathtaking wedding dress, its entire length covered in delicate lace and beadwork. Its design was so intricate it couldn't have been made by human hands alone.

Yet for all the woman's beauty and fine clothes, she was covered from head to toe in black streaks of…something. Soot perhaps, or dried ink. Lily wasn't sure.

She *was* sure, however, of the woman's identity.

"Annabelle Witherspoon," Lily said. It was a statement, not a question.

The woman glared at her. "Who are you and where did you come from?" Her voice had soft, musical undertones, yet she spoke harshly.

Lily raised her hands in a placating gesture. "My name is Lily Singer. I'm a wizard, like you. I'm here because I've been asked to help get rid of the curse you cast on Francis Jackson and his house a hundred years ago. What I want to know is, how did you get here? They buried your body in 1911."

Annabelle had opened her mouth to interrupt, but froze in place at Lily's last statement. Her rosy features blanched white under the dirty smudges covering her skin.

"What did you say?" she whispered, hostility turning to horror.

"I said, they buried your body in 1911. It's been almost a hundred years since you died. What are you? A ghost?" Lily took a step toward the obviously shaken girl; Annabelle looked ready to faint.

"One hundred years..." Annabelle murmured, shock and disbelief in her wide eyes as she slowly sank to her knees, dress pooling around her in slinky folds. "I knew I had been here many weeks, perhaps months, but...a hundred years? That is impossible..."

She looked up at Lily, expression confused, eyes desperately pleading for some sort of reassurance. Sighing, Lily sat cross-legged in front of her and tried to take her hands, unsure if her spectral body could even touch the other wizard. It could. Annabelle's hands felt ice cold, and Lily squeezed them reassuringly, not sure what else to do.

They sat in silence for several moments before Annabelle spoke again, an edge in her voice.

"I suppose this means...he is dead now too?"

Lily didn't need to ask who "he" was. "Yes, sort of. You and he actually died around the same time. But he's still here, as a ghost."

Annabelle looked up sharply, body going rigid and hatred warring with longing for supremacy on her face. In the end, neither won. Both were swept away by the sorrow, sharp and piercing as a sword, that overtook her expression as she burst into tears.

She wept for a long time, body heaving with sobs as she wailed in sorrow and rocked back and forth. Lily felt incredibly awkward intruding on this private moment, but it felt cruel not to offer some sort of comfort. She moved to sit beside the weeping girl and put an arm around her shoulders. Annabelle leaned into her, and there they sat until the girl's storm of grief began to subside.

Once the sobs had faded into sniffles, Lily ventured to speak again.

"I know this is hard, but if we're going to make things right, I need you to tell me what happened. I have much of it worked out, between what Francis told me and what you wrote in your diary. But th—"

"My diary!" Annabelle interrupted, pulling back to look at her. "How did you find it? I had it very well hidden."

"No, you didn't," Lily said, confused. "You left it with all your other belongings in your apartment when you died. It got packed away in a relative's attic, then donated to a local museum, which is where I found it."

"That is…well I…I mean to say it was rather rude of you to read someone else's private writing."

"Not at all," Lily said, a bit stiffly. "You've been dead for a long time. It's no longer personal, it's history."

They were both silent for a moment.

"For what it's worth, it's clear from your writing that you're incredibly skilled. I've learned a lot from the diary, though some of your spells I found rather… reckless."

Annabelle smiled faintly, as if remembering better days.

"Why don't you tell me what happened that night," Lily continued, "then I'll tell you what I know, and we'll figure this out."

The girl was silent for a while, staring at the ground. When she finally spoke, her voice was so soft and halting that Lily had to lean close to hear it.

"When Francis…" she paused and took a shuddering breath, blinking back more tears, "when he informed me we could not be wed, I was so angry, so hurt and betrayed, I called upon the most harmful spell I knew. It was foolhardy, I know, but obviously I was beyond reason at the time. I had never actually tried the spell before, but the theory was sound. Its intention was to bring upon the recipient the same sorrow they had inflicted upon the caster. I had this rather romantic idea that I would leave him miserable for a few months, unable to be happy with anyone else, then he would come crawling back to me on hands and knees, begging me to reconsider. I would magnanimously forgive him and all would be well.

"Yet, something went wrong. I was so furious, so violent in the casting, that I must have thrown too much of myself into the spell. I have thought for endless hours about what happened, and I have decided I must have made the spell too personal. Somehow, I tied part of my soul, my suffering, to the anchor. How else was the spell supposed to accomplish what I commanded, to make Francis suffer what I suffered, without a part of me to fuel it?"

Lily saw it then, the reason Annabelle was never able to dispel the curse, and why she, and therefore Francis, had died. But she kept silent, to let this bit of Annabelle's soul finish her story.

"The last memory I have is completing the spell and releasing it as I threw my ring at that good-for-nothing. Then I blacked out. I woke up here—" she gestured at the shining black mist around them "—in this godforsaken place. There's nothing but mist. It has no end, no walls, no features of any kind. I have walked endlessly and never come upon a single thing but mist. I never tire, hunger, or thirst, as if I am in some kind of stasis. I have had nothing but hatred and hurt to keep me company. It is a wonder I have not gone mad. I should have; I thought I would. But even my moods have disappeared.

"I have tried to escape so many times, but there is no way out. I am cut off from the Source. I can not feel it anymore, or else I would have freed myself long ago."

Annabelle fell silent, and Lily suppressed a shudder. She couldn't imagine the horror of being trapped here, unaware of the world or anything in it, including her own body.

"Tell me, what happened after I cast my spell?" Annabelle asked, shaking off the pall that had come over her. "What happened to Francis? Tell me everything."

So Lily told her, including the cryptic passages at the end of her own diary, written by a part of herself she was cut off from.

"But why was I not able to end the curse?" she asked, brow furrowed in thought. "I have tried often enough from here, and you said myself 'out there' tried as well."

Lily thought about that. "If you're cut off from the Source here, then a piece of your soul separated from 'you' outside would have nothing to draw on. You said yourself you couldn't cast magic. There's no way you'd be able to undo the curse from in here."

"But what about my other self? I don't see how a part of my soul being stuck here would stop me…her…us."

Lily smiled sadly. "You never knew it, Annabelle, but you cast a curse you could never break yourself. You have no magic in here, and because a part of you was stuck here, even though the rest of you met all the parameters, she could never break it herself either."

"Parameters? What do you mean?" Annabelle asked, bewildered.

"To end the curse, you have to forgive the one who wronged you," Lily said, gently. "Francis said you spoke more words of power after you threw the ring, after part of your soul split off. So you 'here' was never aware of the extra clause you 'there' added on."

Annabelle looked at her, even more confused.

"Ga-arhus-a," Lily said, speaking Enkinim. "Forgiveness. You wrote it in your diary, near the end. You said you'd forgiven him, yet the spell wouldn't go away."

Realization dawned on Annabelle's face. "I couldn't forgive him, because only part of me ever tried."

"Exactly," Lily confirmed.

Annabelle got up abruptly, turning her back on Lily and crossing her arms.

"Annabelle?" Lily asked, tentatively, getting up herself. "You *are* going to forgive him, aren't you?"

"You have no idea what it's been like," Annabelle said softly, not turning, "being stuck here. That bastard threw me away like a piece of trash, and all I've been able to do for the past century is relive that betrayal over and over again." Her voice broke.

Lily felt helpless. She was the last person in the world qualified to resolve interpersonal conflict, especially since she still resented her mother for concealing her magical heritage. Who was she to talk about forgiveness? But she had to try.

"Look, Annabelle," she began. "I can't begin to imagine how much pain you've been through. But you haven't been able to see the pain Francis has suffered—"

"Good!" Annabelle exclaimed, whirling with hands on hips in a defiant stance. "He deserves it."

Lily sighed, at a loss. She knew forgiveness should well from a generous heart, not be based on merit. But such abstract principles wouldn't appeal to an angry fragment of soul chained by unresolved hurt. If only she could get this part of Annabelle to feel pity or remorse. "Does he really deserve it?" she finally asked. "I know he broke your heart. But hearts heal. Your curse killed him, Annabelle. It *killed* him and his whole family. His parents, his wife...even his newborn child."

Annabelle gasped, tears forming in her eyes again. Lily continued, relentless.

"He has paid for his sins and then some. And he's *sorry*. So, so, sorry. He told me himself. He said he acted in a cowardly and reprehensible fashion, and was eternally ashamed of what he did. His greatest regret has been never getting to apologize to you, to make things right."

Tears streamed down Annabelle's dirty face, though they did not cut lines through the grime. It was as if the dirt on her skin was evidence of something deeper, something inside, that simple tears could not wash away.

Lily stepped forward and took Annabelle's cold hands in her own. "He knows you cast the curse, but he has never blamed you for it or held it against you. He has forgiven *you*, but he'll never be at peace until you forgive *him*. His soul has been adrift, unable to pass on, for a hundred years because of all this hurt between you. The only way either of you will ever be free is if you forgive him. Your hatred is a heavy chain, holding you tight to your torment. You have to let go, or you'll stay here, reliving that hurt, forever."

She fell silent, surprised at the intensity of her own words. Annabelle stared her straight in the eye, expression longing once again.

"I think you want to forgive him," Lily said very softly. "So why don't you?"

Annabelle took a shuddering breath, then nodded slowly, hesitantly.

Lily smiled, took Annabelle's other hand and pulled her close, so that their foreheads touched, cold spirit to warm flesh. Closing her eyes, Lily drew upon the Source and together they spoke the words that would complete the curse's reversal, "ga-arhus-a ken": *it is forgiven.*

At those words, the black mist surrounding them exploded into light, and a gale wind arose, buffeting their bodies. As Lily tightened her hold on Annabelle's hands, she yelled a question, but the whipping wind all but tore her words away. Everything around them seemed to be compressing, collapsing in. But, unlike Annabelle, Lily was not a sliver of soul, cut off and trapped. She was a whole person, and her body was her anchor. With a gut-wrenching yank, she felt herself pulled backward, out of the whirlwind and toward herself, dragging Annabelle's specter with her. Suddenly, the wind was gone, and darkness returned.

Lily opened her eyes to a strange sight. Floating, she looked down and saw her own body, motionless, cross-legged on the floor, just where she'd left it. In her body's hands was the ring, its engraved runes blazing with a white fire as the last of the clinging, black mist that had permeated the house was sucked into it. Around her everything was dark, but not from mist. It was the soft, moonlit darkness of night. She could see out the open front doors to where Sebastian had apparently been pacing, but now stood frozen mid-step, mouth open, eyes shocked.

"Wha—?" he started to say.

Lily ignored him, knowing how little time was left. Through the insubstantial grip she had on Annabelle's hands, she could feel the piece of soul pulling, trying to dissipate, kept in place only by Lily's magical hold. Annabelle seemed oblivious to this, however, as her eyes fixed on something behind Lily.

Lily smiled to herself and floated to the side, keeping a firm hold on one of Annabelle's hands, even as she felt the pull increase. She fought to hold on, to give the girl a chance to say goodbye.

"Annabelle?" Francis's ghostly voice cracked, and big, swelling tears as white as pearls slipped down his cheeks as he took in the sight of his lost love, clothed in a wedding dress she never got to wear for him. He floated there, hesitant and unsure.

Smiling broadly now, Lily tugged on Annabelle's hand, pulling her toward Francis's incorporeal embrace and noticing as she did that the girl was now free of black streaks and her dress was as pure white as the moonlight shining outside. Annabelle drifted forward, reaching out with her free hand to trace the lines of Francis's face, her wide-eyed gaze full of wonder.

They both glowed faintly in the darkness, taking in each other, at a loss for words.

"I'm so sorry," Francis whispered, voice trembling with emotion as it broke the silence between them.

"I know," Annabelle said simply, smiling through her tears. "And…I forgive you."

A look of joyous peace came over the ghost's face, probably for the first time since he died, and he smiled. Truly smiled.

Annabelle pulled her hand out of Lily's grasp, and Lily let her go, knowing it was time. The ghost and the bit of soul wrapped their arms around each other, now released from a hundred years of hurt, and their glowing forms began to fade.

As they did, Francis spoke one last time, looking at Lily over his love's shoulder. "Thank you. You are both mighty in magic and mighty in heart. I hope those occult books I collected all those years ago do you some good. I could never make heads or tails of them. Goodbye, Lily Singer."

"Goodbye," Lily whispered, feeling a single tear slip down her cheek.

Even as the last of their glow faded into nothingness, Lily felt her ghostlike body lurch. Startled, she looked below her and saw the ring was blazing white with light and vibrating violently. The curse had been unmade, and now all that power had to go somewhere.

She didn't even have time to brace herself as the ring exploded.

The blast of pure magic slammed her discarnate self back into her body with a painful wrench as her personal ward flickered, taking the brunt of the abuse. In a second, it was over.

Shocked by the sudden influx of stimuli from her five senses, she groaned and straightened from her hunched position. Glancing down at her hands, she relaxed her death grip on the now crumbling powder that had once been a ring, and flexed her stiff fingers.

There was a sound of running footsteps, then Sebastian was kneeling beside her, hand on her shoulder.

"Are you alright? Is everything okay? Heck, I was so worried!"

Lily tried to chuckle, but coughed instead, throat as dry as paper. She swallowed a few times and tried again.

"Why? I was only gone fifteen minutes or so. Thirty at most."

Sebastian looked at her funny; she could see his expression faintly in the blackness. "Look around you, Lil. It's nighttime. You've been sitting here for nine hours, hunched over that ring. You went all cold and stiff, but I was afraid to wake you, in case it made things worse. If something hadn't happened soon, I was going to call—" he paused, as if what he was about to say pained him "—my great-aunt."

Lily was so shocked she forgot to tell him off for using her nickname. "How is that possible? I wasn't gone that long." Then it hit her. "That's why Annabelle thought only a few months had passed. Time must be different in...wher-ever we were. Maybe it actually was stasis...wait, your great-aunt? I don't believe it. You were really going to call Madam Barrington?"

Sebastian made a face and ignored her incredulity. "For-get it. You're awake, so it's a moot point. Now stop spouting nonsense and tell me what happened."

But Lily ignored his question, suddenly remembering the blast of magic. She looked him up and down, worriedly searching for any sign of harm.

"Are *you* okay? That was a pretty big explosion."

Sebastian waved her concern away. "I'm fine, but that shield you gave me isn't." He dug in his pocket and pulled out the blacked and cracked pieces of the clay tablet she'd given him.

Lily relaxed, relieved. "I'm so glad you had it on you."

"Come on, Lil, I'm not that stupid. I've learned to expect the worst when hanging around you. You always manage to blow things up."

Lily glared at him but couldn't remain angry long. A grin spread involuntarily over her face. The curse was bro-ken, all hurts healed, and the house returned to normal. She noticed that, with Francis gone, warmth had rushed back into the great hall from the summer night outside. Sebas-tian helped her up and they stood, enjoying the night air as a cacophony of cricket song filled the empty house with music.

Epilogue

Lily sat at her desk, staring at the copy of Annabelle's diary as it lay beside her eduba. It was once again past two in the morning, though this time because the drive back from the Jackson Mansion was so long, not because she'd stayed up reading.

Once back in Atlanta, she'd had to drop Sebastian off at his house before driving home. She'd barely remembered to insist on some money to cover gas before letting him exit the car. It had been like prying a cell phone away from a teenager: incredibly difficult and apt to leave the subject sulky afterwards. Sebastian would live. He was getting paid, after all, for the job. He could charge his employer for the travel expense.

When she finally got home, she found Sir Kipling waiting for her inside the door. He managed to almost trip her an impressive six times between the front door and the kitchen, all in a furious attempt to fully coat her pant legs with fur.

Now she sat at her desk, freshly showered and wrapped in a fuzzy bathrobe, staring at the diary and quite unable to sleep. She couldn't shake the image of Francis's face when Annabelle had forgiven him. He'd experienced such relief, such joy, it made her think uncomfortably of her mother. They'd parted on…less than friendly terms, to say the least. There'd been a lot of yelling, mostly on her part. Did her mother hurt inside, even as Francis had, because of their parting words? Was she just like Annabelle, trapped by her own hurt and resentment? She hadn't been home in seven years, since she left for college. She didn't like to admit it, especially to herself, but she missed her family. An empty hole gaped in her heart where they should have been, but couldn't be. They didn't even know her. Her stepfamily had no idea who she really was because they were mundane, and her wizard family had no idea who she was because her mother had cut them off for reasons she refused to discuss.

Forgiveness wasn't going to get her anywhere; it wouldn't make her less empty. She could forgive her mother, but would that really set her free? What she wanted was answers—the truth—and she was going to find it. Maybe once she'd discovered her past and found her father, then she could put it all behind her. If she spoke to her mother now, she'd just get angry again at her refusal to tell the truth. Deep down, a part of her knew she ought to pick up the phone anyway. But something held her back.

She shook her head, trying to dislodge that uncomfortable train of thought.

There was one other thing that kept her awake as well, and she concentrated on that. It was something Annabelle had said. Lily had meant to ask her fellow wizard a myriad of questions about her magic, methods, and family line, but had only remembered in time to ask one thing before they'd both been pulled out of the ring: Who had been her mentor?

Annabelle's reply, barely audible over the rush of wind, had been, "Ask the fae."

At least, that's what Lily thought she'd said. It might have been "ask *le* fae," she wasn't sure.

Lily sat and considered Annabelle's words for a long while, trying to puzzle out their meaning. Then she opened her eduba and began the process of summoning every reference to the fae she could find.

She was no longer a clueless country girl from an Alabama backwater, but being a library archivist with no knowledge of her past wasn't much better. She was a wizard but still knew next to nothing about her culture, her people, or her family history. How could she decide who to become if she didn't even know who she was now?

Well, it was time to do some research, starting with the fae.

Interlude

Chasing Rabbits

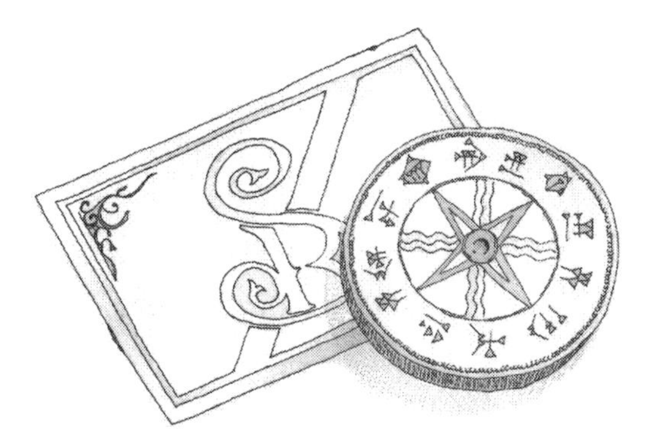

Sebastian Blackwell liked to think of himself as a pretty decent person. He obeyed the law—mostly—and helped people out when they were in a tight spot. What more could anyone ask? He was no saint, he knew, but even he deserved a bit of respect.

So why was it that, after giving his old school buddy a place to crash, he got this in return?

Standing in the middle of his wrecked house, he surveyed the damage. Admittedly, the house didn't look much more trashed than usual—he had a unique sense of interior decorating. But when you knew where each little thing was in your own personal mess, it was quite distressing to have someone else rearrange it. And rearranged it was, not to mention ransacked. His stash of cash, his father's watch, some electronics, and every other valuable-looking item that was small enough to carry was gone.

Worse, though, was his sock drawer. You never really knew what it felt like to be violated until someone went rooting through your sock drawer looking for valuables. And, like any sane male, that was exactly where he'd been keeping his. Including the artifact. Curse it all. Cory would pay. He'd thought that little scumbag had been drunk to the point of passing out and therefore virtually harmless—minus the vomit, that is. No one that drunk could have made off with so much stuff. Which meant he'd been faking it, relying on Sebastian's good-naturedness and planning all along to turn around and rob him blind.

Sebastian's fingers twitched restlessly as he resisted the urge to punch something. All he'd ever wanted was to make his parents proud: do the right thing, help people, follow their example. But whenever he tried to apply that to the real world, things like this happened. How had they managed it?

He sighed and bent to pick up a pile of magazines. There was no use crying over spilt milk, so he got busy rearranging the mess back to its proper place. The quicker he cleaned up, the quicker he could get to the important part: tracking down a scumbag.

"Hey, where did you get that watch?" Sebastian asked as he pointed, leaning on the glass counter of Lucky's Pawn Shop, one of many in metro Atlanta.

The burly shop owner glanced at him from where he bent, rearranging gold rings in a neighboring case. He surveyed the timepiece for a moment as he considered. "Fella brought it in a week back."

Sebastian's lips thinned to a hard line. "Short, scrawny guy? Kinda shifty looking?"

The shop owner straightened and closed his ring case, coming to loom over Sebastian across the counter. "Maybe. What's it to you?" He had that I'm-not-threatening-you-yet-but-just-give-me-a-reason look on his face.

Sebastian put both hands in his pockets and shrugged, attempting to seem less threatening. "Just curious. Did the guy bring in anything else?" As he asked, he curled his fingers around his truth coin—an intricately carved disk of silver the size of a half-dollar that he'd inherited from his father. The coin grew warm whenever someone lied.

"Na. Just that piece," the burly man said, crossing his arms. "You lookin' for somethin'?"

Truth. Sebastian raised an eyebrow, resisting the urge to scowl. This was the only thing of his he'd found after a whole week trawling Atlanta's pawnshops. He'd already tapped his contacts, none of whom had fish as small as Cory on their radar. He'd figured Cory would have run to the first pawnshop he could find and unloaded his loot, but the little git had had more sense than that. And now Sebastian had to buy back his own watch, which left an extremely sour taste in his mouth. "Yeah," he finally replied, "how much for it?" He pointed again at his father's watch. As he did, he concentrated, hiding a smile of satisfaction when a slight shimmer, visible only to him, appeared on the watch.

The shop owner eyed him. "Two hundred."

Sebastian snorted. "Yeah, right. That piece of junk is a fake. You can tell from the discoloration on all the wear points. And check out those scratches. Nobody would touch this for more than fifty, and only then if they liked beat-up swag."

The man glanced down at the watch and did a double take, staring as if he'd never seen it before. When he looked back up, he attempted a poker face but was only partially successful. Sebastian could still see the confusion in his eyes. "My guy checks every piece that comes in here," he said, as if reassuring himself. "We don't take fakes."

Sebastian's coin was cool in his hand. The man was telling the truth, which Sebastian already knew because the watch was his in the first place, and most certainly real. Yet, his illusion had shaken the man. Made him unsure.

Sebastian leaned in close. "Look. I get it. You're just trying to make a living. But we both know there are always fakes. Why not? Most schmucks can't tell the difference, ignorance is bliss and all that. But anybody can see how beat up this thing is. How about I give you fifty cash and you won't have to worry about someone callin' you on it."

"I can do hundred-fifty cash, but that's highway robbery," the man said, glancing back down at the watch as if to check that it still looked worn.

"Yeah, highway robbery of me! Come on, seventy-five, let's shake on it," Sebastian said, extending his hand.

The store owner stared at him, torn. "Hundred even. And don't show your ugly mug in here again. At this rate you'll run me outta business."

"Will do," Sebastian replied, grim, and handed over the cash. He was still mad as a hornet at having to pay for his own belongings, so he didn't feel any guilt at using fae glamour on the man. The fact that he himself wasn't fae, only using borrowed skills, meant his illusions had to be small and the changes subtle. But it was a useful trick. Which, unfortunately, was no help in figuring out where Cory had sold his artifact. At this point, there was only one more lead to try before he called in the cavalry. He hoped it worked, since he would be exceedingly annoyed if he had to resort to using Grimmold.

★ ★ ★ ★

Sebastian knocked, then took a step back to let the flimsy screen door swing shut. He stood on the crumbling concrete steps of a house in south Atlanta that belonged to a mutual "friend" of his and Cory's, Fester Jones. When he said *friend*, he actually meant *enabling low-life*, but then Cory was an adult and had every right to choose his own associates. The only thing he and Fester had in common was that they both tried to keep Cory alive: he because he'd once known a decent guy named Cory and felt obligated to that memory; Fester because Cory made a good drinking buddy. Once upon a time, Cory had been one of those rich kids too naive to recognize danger and too stupid to stay away from it when it was pointed out. As a thrill-seeking teenager, he'd gotten hooked on gambling and alcohol. That was the beginning of the end. Family fortune went down the drain and he became a shadow of himself.

This house was where Sebastian, one night long ago, had dropped off a very drunk Cory after saving him from a couple of thugs he was mouthing off to. Cory told him, between vomits out the window, to take him to his ol' pal Fester. Sebastian had helped a stumbling Cory to the door, handed him off to Fester, and hoped it was the last time he'd ever darken Fester's door. It was not. Fast-forward many years, and, knowing Cory had long ago been estranged from the few family members he had left, this was the only place he could think of where Cory might go to ground.

Fester, when he finally answered the door, looked sleepy, though it was already noon and the hot summer sun was high in the sky. His jersey and shorts hung off his wasted frame, showing the effects of drug and alcohol addiction. Clearly visible on flabby arms and legs were an assortment of tattoos. Fester peered at him through the screen, expression hovering between caution and annoyance. "What d'ya want?"

Hand curled around his coin, Sebastian decided on a direct route. "I'm Sebastian. Remember me? Friend of Cory's? I'm looking for him. You seen him recently?"

Though it was hard to tell through the screen door, Fester's body language seemed to shift from sleepy to alert as soon as the name "Cory" was mentioned.

"Who's askin'?" he hedged, not answering Sebastian's question.

"Just me," Sebastian shrugged, keeping cool, though he was starting to get the impression Cory was caught up in more trouble than the idiot could handle. Again. "He borrowed something of mine I need back. Just trying to find him."

The man started stuttering nervously and tried to close the door. "You g—got the wrong house. I ain't never hearda Cory. Never s—seen you before neither."

But Sebastian, hand smarting from the sudden blaze of heat such falsehoods caused in his coin, opened the screen in time to get his toe in the door, keeping it from closing. "Come on, man. You're lying, I know you're lying, and now you know I know you're lying. I'm not out to hurt anyone, I just want my stuff back. If he's not here, where could I find him?"

Slowly, the door opened wide enough for Fester to peer at him from the darkness within, silently considering Sebastian's words. Finally he said, "I ain't s—seen him in a spell, but if he shows, I'll tell him you came l—lookin'. Best bet for findin' him is same as always." Fester tried again to shut the door, obviously assuming Sebastian knew what he meant. Unfortunately, Sebastian knew all too well, and his coin was too ambiguously warm to give him an excuse to grill the man any more.

"Just give me a call if you hear from him, okay?" Sebastian said, keeping his foot in the door and holding out a piece of paper with his number on it. As Fester hesitantly extended his hand to take it, Sebastian noticed a fresh tattoo on the inside of his wrist forming the stylized letters "SLB."

Great, just what he needed in his life. Gangs.

Four nights and twice as many illegal gambling rooms later, Sebastian was not sure he'd be able to resist choking Cory to death when he finally found the little wretch. From pawnshops to drug-infested neighborhoods to alcohol-ridden back rooms, he was going through an enormous amount of trouble to find one alcoholic gambling addict. At times he considered giving up, mostly because he could barely stand the sorry lowlives he had to rub elbows with to find all of Cory's favorite spots. Pretending to be one of them grated on all his sensibilities—not that he had many, but there were a few. He had to employ every ounce of charm, wit, and skullduggery he possessed to stay one step ahead. A few witchy tricks didn't hurt, but he generally tried to save those for when he really needed them. Unlike high and mighty wizards, who had a bottomless pit of magic to call on—the Source or whatever impressive-sounding name they used—his resources were limited. When you lived off tricks and favors, you learned to make do.

Good ol' Lil was the only decent wizard he'd met. He'd long ago decided it was because she hadn't grown up being taught she was better than mundanes. She hadn't even known she was a wizard until a few years before he met her. She was just a normal, shy southern gal and that was fine with him, mostly because her naiveté was so adorable. He'd considered asking for her help to find Cory but couldn't bring himself to involve her in all this. She was just so innocent.

Not like him, not after what he'd done as a teenager; he'd never been the same after that. Not that it wasn't entirely his own fault. He knew he'd never be rid of his past, so he just cleaned up his act as best he could. His goal was to be someone his parents could be proud of, even if they'd never have approved of his methods. So what if his ancestors were rolling in their graves at the thought of a Blackwell being a witch? If he used his abilities for good, what did it matter? And getting back that artifact was definitely good, if the stories he'd overheard his father telling were any indicator.

And so he relied on his street smarts as much as possible, pushing on from back room to back room. Yet watching the greed—or worse, the deadness—behind every pair of eyes he faced was almost more than he could take. It was the slow and inevitable knowledge that alcohol, drugs, and poverty were grinding their lives into dust and they'd given up caring.

The problem with quitting was that the sorry, low-life addict he was looking for had once been a friend. The other problem was that said erstwhile friend had stolen a treasured family heirloom. Even if Sebastian wasn't sure what it was or what to do with it, he had to get it back.

The picture that finally started to form indicated Cory had not been seen for several weeks, which was odd for an addict. People with those kinds of habits tended to stick to a certain turf, and the fact that Cory had abandoned his meant one of two things: he was dead or he was hiding out. The tough part was finding out which. It was a toss-up, what with the number of people he came across who scowled at

Cory's name, muttering angrily at all the money he owed them.

Yet there was one person who didn't scowl, and that got Sebastian's attention.

He was sitting at yet another bar, nursing yet another cheap beer. It wasn't that he didn't like alcohol, he was just more of a bourbon and spiced rum kind of guy. But he needed his wits about him, so watered-down beer it was. Light in the bar was almost nonexistent, making the whole establishment a dark den of smoke and hopeless faces, there to drown their sorrows and forget how awful their lives were. This wasn't one of the back-room gambling houses, just a normal bar. But it was in a neighborhood known for illegal gambling and, according to the last place he'd visited, Cory's favorite drinking spot. Personally, Sebastian didn't get what his friend saw in the place. Everything was either chipped, bent, wobbly, or simply cheap, and there wasn't even a pool table.

The patrons looked no better. Being late in the evening—early in the morning, rather—only the faithful alcoholics and newbies so plastered they couldn't find their way out were still around. Sebastian was scoping the place out by examining everyone's reflection in the bar's mirror, allowing him to stare at each person in turn without raising suspicion. To get information, he'd found it worked best to pick the loneliest-looking sod and strike up a conversation, making friends before bringing up Cory's name. Or, even better, get friendly with the bartender.

This place's bartender was the kind he liked to get friendly with. Short and cute, but not so pretty that every guy in the bar would be glowering at his back if he spoke to her. She might have been called plain by some, but Sebastian could see she still had a bit of life behind her eyes and that made her appearance shine in a way no amount of curves or makeup could. It was rare in these sorts of places.

He watched her surreptitiously as she cleaned glasses nearby. Finally judging the moment was right, he opened his mouth to deliver an irresistible one-liner, but she beat him to the chase.

"Save it for the girl over at table nine. Figure she needs it more'n me," she said, not even looking at him.

He glanced in the mirror, estimating the target of her comment by the angle of her chin thrust. The woman at table nine did indeed look like she needed a pickup line, or really any line at all. But he was no knight in shining armor here to save a damsel in distress—even the thought made him snort. No, he was on a mission. So he took a sip of beer, hid a grimace, and tried again.

"She might need it more than you, but I wasn't looking for someone who needed it. Those are dime a dozen. I was looking for someone who deserved it." He showed her his best charming smile, making sure it leaned more toward sincerity than flattery. She obviously didn't respond to the latter and her comment indicated a dearth in her life of the former.

It worked. Or at least, it got her to look at him, a small smile twitching her lips. "Well, ain't you a sweetie. I'd almost believe you, too, if it weren't the same line I wager you put to every pretty lady you talk to." She bent to put away the glasses she'd finished drying, then straightened to start on more.

"Well, since you're honest enough to admit you're pretty, but humble enough to know you're not the only one, I think you can tell the difference between truth and a lie," he countered, grinning. Taking another swig of beer, he casually withdrew his silver coin from his pocket and started rolling it back and forth over his knuckles, waiting for a reply.

The girl grinned at his brashness and shook her head in amused disbelief but was called away by another customer before she could respond.

Sebastian could wait. He sat patiently, playing with his coin and pretending to nurse his beer until she returned to cleaning glasses.

Finally, she broke the silence. "What's a guy like you doing in a place like this?"

"I could ask the same of you."

"Well, when your daddy owns the bar…" she trailed off, smiling at the slightly stricken look on Sebastian's face. "Family's all we got in these parts. Gotta be tighta than glue."

"You won that one," he joked, holding up both hands in a sign of surrender and momentarily tucking his coin—still as cool as glass—between thumb and palm, before going back to walking it over his hand.

"So you still ain't answered my question. I'm curious now, 'cause only two kindsa people drink that stuff." She indicated his beer bottle. "Poor folk an' those too dumb to know betta. You don't strike me as either."

Sebastian grinned. "What an astute mind you have. Since you ask, I'm looking for a friend. Not having much luck, either."

The girl lowered her eyes, focusing on the glass she was drying. When she spoke, her voice was quiet and careful. "Usually when people be looking for someone, they up to trouble. What kinda trouble you chasing down in my establishment?"

Despite himself, Sebastian chuckled. "Ironically, you're right in this case. The trouble I'm chasing down is called Cory, and if I ever get my hands on his sorry—" he stopped, seeing the girl glance up involuntarily at the sound of Cory's name. But she immediately looked back down, hiding her expression. Changing tack, he sighed. "He's caused me enough trouble I have every right to beat him black and blue. But if I could just know he's safe and not lying in a ditch somewhere, I'd be happy."

"Sounds like y'all've had a rough time of it," she said, probing cautiously.

"You have no idea," Sebastian said, about to lean back and drape his arm casually over the back of his chair before remembering he was on a barstool. He settled for leaning on one elbow, eyes on his marching coin while he watched the girl out of the corner of his eye. "We were high school buddies, but he's done nothing but get himself into trouble since then. We're not real close, but I pull him out of the deep end now and then, if you know what I mean. Only, he's gone missing and I've worried myself sick looking for him. Blond, scrawny guy who couldn't punch through wet paper. Has a terrible gambling and drinking addiction." Having had years to practice telling only the parts of the truth he wanted people to know, rather than outright lies, his coin stayed nice and cool as he recounted his woes to the pretty bartender.

She seemed more interested in his story than was normal. Absentmindedly still drying the same glass over and over, she bit her lip. Her searching look made him even more certain she knew Cory, liked him, and was now trying to decide if it was safe to tell what she knew. What Cory could have done to gain the favor of a cute, smart girl in a tough place like this he had no idea. But it was nice to know he wasn't the only person who cared if the idiot was alive or dead. He didn't like the man, but he didn't wish him harm. Well maybe a little harm, but nothing fatal.

With deliberate motions, the girl finally put the thoroughly dry glass away and nodded. "I mighta seen a guy like that around. Not recently though. An' that's got me worried..." she paused, thinking. "Bar closes in thirty. Gimme a few after that to clean the place up, then meet me out front."

Though curious as to why they couldn't talk then and there, he kept his mouth shut and nodded. Flipping his coin, he snatched it out of the air and stashed it back in his pocket. It had stayed cool through their entire conversation. So much truth was refreshing, but he liked what he heard less and less. The one person not angry with Cory was too nervous to talk about him in public. He wondered what Cory had gotten himself into.

At closing, Sebastian shuffled out with the rest of the sleepy or drunk patrons. While they dispersed up and down the sidewalk, he crossed the street and climbed into his car, locking the doors. With the closest street light unsurprisingly dark—the city had more important things to do than maintain streetlights, after all—Sebastian was able to slouch down in his seat and be confident no one looking at his car would see him. Usually an empty car in such a neighborhood would be in danger of a jacking. But Sebastian drove a beat-up clunker for that very reason. Keeping it full of trash and smelly pizza boxes helped too. Nobody wanted it but him, and that's just the way he liked it.

About ten minutes later, the lights in the bar flickered off and the pretty bartender came out, turning to lock the door behind her. The girl had never actually offered her name, though neither had he, come to think of it. He was considering this when he saw a dark shape approach. There was one working streetlight within view, but it cast such poor illumination over the scene it may as well have been off. When the dark shape stopped by the girl instead of continuing onward, Sebastian sat upright, body tensing.

The two figures spoke in low voices. It was obvious they weren't strangers. Sebastian was just starting to relax when the dark shape, now revealed in the faint lamplight to be a man, took hold of the girl's arm and raised his voice. The girl protested sharply, tugging against the man's grip and trying to back up, but he was much bigger than she.

Before he could think about it rationally, Sebastian was out of his car and crossing the street. Despite his car's age, the door hinges were well oiled and he left the door open, so there was no noise to alert the attacker of his approach. His brief hope of settling the argument with a few choice words were dashed when the man drew back his free hand and slapped the girl full in the face. The force of his blow whipped her head around and Sebastian could see the tears in her eyes as they shimmered in the dim lamplight.

Then he was on them and delivering a series of swift jabs to the man's rib cage, causing him to hunch over in pain, letting go of the girl and turning to face his attacker. Yet the man raised his hands too late to block Sebastian's solid punch to his nose. Sebastian heard the crunch of cartilage and felt the pain on his knuckles even as the man reeled back, howling in pain. Putting himself between the angry man and the bartender, Sebastian started whispering. "Elwa Pilanti'ara. Pip, you listening? A full bottle of Captain Morgan and as many cocktail cherries as you can eat if you chase this sorry excuse for a human until he drops. Deal?"

From somewhere above his head there was a tinkling laugh and what sounded like "wheeee" that moved quickly toward the man picking himself up off the pavement. Sebastian saw that he'd made the right choice, and only just in time. As the man reached behind him for what could only have been a gun, he suddenly yelped and slapped a hand to his ear. Sebastian heard the laugh again, from this distance sounding like the squeaking chirp of a hummingbird. The sound brought a wicked grin to his face, though from the man's continuing yells, he didn't share Sebastian's mirth.

The man was now waving his arms around his head as if trying to fend off a cloud of mosquitoes or a dive-bombing bird. In addition to the stream of blood coming from his nose, Sebastian saw pricks of blood on the man's forehead, cheeks, and arms, as though something with tiny claws had been raking him. It was actually rather impressive how long the man stuck it out, slapping wildly about him with one hand while attempting to draw his weapon with the other. Each time he gave up with a yell, using both hands to snatch desperately at whatever was tormenting him. Finally, either his bravery or stupidity gave out. Swearing and throwing choice obscenities over his shoulder, he turned and high-tailed it down the sidewalk, arms still waving about him. Little did he know that nothing would save him from what had been set in motion. Not until he dropped to the ground in exhaustion would his tormentor return to Sebastian to collect the promised payment. Sebastian tried not to feel too pleased with himself.

"Wha—what was that?" a scared voice asked behind him.

Whirling, Sebastian cursed himself for forgetting the girl. "Nothing. I just gave him a good pounding. Probably never had to deal with getting his butt handed to him on a platter before, and went bonkers. You okay? Let me take a look at that." He drew closer to examine the girl's face, knowing he couldn't explain his unorthodox methods. What would he say? That he had a soft spot for the fae? Not even most witches would understand, much less this girl.

The girl put up a reassuring hand, brushing him off as she touched her own face lightly, wincing. "No, it's alright. Skin ain't broke, just a bruise. What you did though…that wasn't nothing. I heard something squeaking, like a mouse. But it was flyin', an'….there was this little green light…" she trailed off, staring up into his face.

Sebastian cursed inwardly. Most mundanes couldn't see fae—not unless the fae revealed themselves on purpose. But sometimes they saw the markers of their presence, if they were actually paying attention. He shrugged, trying to play it off. "Really? I didn't hear anything but that guy yelling."

"Yeah, there was definitely something there. Who are you?" The girl drew back, eyes searching his face in the dim light.

"Just a regular guy trying to keep some thug from hitting a girl," Sebastian said, shifting uncomfortably and sticking his hands in his pockets. He wasn't one to hide who he was, just selective about when and where he advertised it. Cute bartenders weren't exactly his customer demographic, and he'd counted on the confusion and darkness to obscure his actions. Apparently this bartender had more than her fair share of curiosity. It reminded him of Lily, which made him smile.

"Look, I'd love to stand here chatting, but I don't have a death wish. That guy might come back with his buddies. Is there somewhere safe I can take you?"

She nodded, still looking shell-shocked. "My apartment's jus' down the street."

Guiding her to his car, he apologized for the trash and settled her into the passenger seat. She directed him several blocks down to a sorry-looking bit of project housing and he escorted her up to her apartment on the second floor, eyes scanning every dark corner for threats.

Her apartment was so small he suspected she only had it to get away from an overbearing family. Just because family should stick together didn't mean they all needed to share the same living space. Despite its size it was tidy, with cheery yellow curtains framing the only window and a few fake flowers in a vase on the tiny excuse for a kitchen table.

The girl got out two cokes, holding one to her bruised face and handing him the other. Nodding in thanks, he took it. When she gestured for him to sit at the cramped table, he politely declined, leaning against the kitchen counter instead as he opened his coke and sipped contentedly. Finally, a girl who knew how to treat a guy. Not that he didn't appreciate Lily's excellent baking skills. But seriously, did she ever drink anything but tea?

Sitting down at the tiny table, the girl rubbed the un-bruised side of her face vigorously before opening her own drink and taking a long swig. With a sigh of contentment, she held it back up to her bruise and looked at Sebastian. "Well, seein' as how you're in my apartment an' like as saved my life, we'd best introduce ourselves afore anything else. I'm Pearl Harris."

"And I'm Sebastian Blackwell. A pleasure to meet you, ma'am," he said, holding out a hand to shake hers.

"Don't you 'ma'am' me," she said with a grin, grasping his hand firmly. Despite her small size, Pearl had quite a grip. "An' thank you for saving me. That was my ex. He won't take a hint, but I never figured he'd..." she stopped, eyes distant and sad, then shook her head. "It don't matter. He's gone now, and I owe you. Least I can do is help you find Cory. He was such a sweetheart, I can't imagine anyone hurtin' him."

Sebastian scratched his head. "Well, I'm glad you see that in him, because the last time I saw him he ransacked my house."

"No!" Pearl gasped, sitting up straight in shock. "Something terrible musta happened for him to do a thing like that."

"I'll say," Sebastian growled. "But honestly I'm tired of helping him. No matter what anyone does, he goes right back to the bottle and gambling. I should've known better than to let him in my house. He's probably in a lot of debt and stole my things to pay someone off. It's a douchebag thing to do, but I understand being in a tight spot. Been there a few times myself. Problem is, he took a family heirloom that's rather…well let's just say it's very important to me. I need it back. That's why I'm trying to find him. And of course to make sure he's still alive," he amended at the look of disapproval on Pearl's face.

Her expression softened, and she sighed deeply. Sebastian recognized that look. It was the look of helpless sadness you felt when someone you cared about was in trouble, but you could do nothing to help. Not because you didn't try, but because they refused to change the habits that got them into trouble in the first place.

"Look, why don't you tell me what you know, and maybe that will help me find him. I'll make sure he's okay and help in any way I can." His coin, pressed against his leg by the material of his pants, warmed only slightly. He wouldn't kill Cory, that was for sure. And he didn't expect to ever see his money again. If only he got that artifact back, he would consider them even. That was helping, right?

Pearl searched his face and was apparently satisfied with what she saw, because she leaned back in her chair and started talking, taking sips of her coke between sentences. "Cory's been comin' 'round to my family's bar for a few years now. A real regular, that one. He ain't always there the same day or time, but he always comes. He's a quiet drunk, an' a sad one. He jus' nurses his drink in a corner, or up at the bar, real quiet like. Sometimes, though, he needs someone to talk to, so we'd talk. Bless his heart, he's likely the sweetest fool I ever met, 'cause he can't keep his trap shut when he's got the drink in him. He's told me all about everything, his gambling debts, his life 'afore all this, even one of his friends. Tall, dark gent named Seb." She smiled up at him, eyes twinkling for a moment. Then she cast her eyes down to her coke, lost back in her memories. "Anyhow, I listened. Told him I cared. Shared some of my own sorrows. We grew close. He dreamt of gettin' outta gambling an' drinking, I dreamt of gettin' outta that bar. But every day, he was there, and so was I.

"But one time, 'bout two weeks ago, he came in all agitated. Usually he's pretty laid back, easygoing, you know? But that night he took fright at every lil' thing. Jumpy as a mouse. He tol' me he'd done something real bad, got in with the wrong crowd. But soon he was gonna fix it an' never have to worry again, he said."

Sebastian raised an eyebrow. "Did you get any more specifics?"

"Here an' there," Pearl said, nodding. "His words was all jumbled, he was so nervous. But sounded like he'd been running drugs to pay off debts an' had figured out a scheme to pay 'em all off an' go away someplace safe."

"Hmm...I don't like the sound of that," Sebastian commented. "Only way he could do that would be stealing or scamming. Then he'd have to run. That would explain his disappearance."

Pearl nodded. "Sounds 'bout right."

"Did he ever say who he was working for?"

Looking furtively back and forth, probably at the paper-thin walls of her cheap apartment, Pearl leaned in and whispered, "Southland Brothers." Sebastian's ears pricked, and things started to make sense. "Round here, though, we call 'em Southland Bastards. They ain't the biggest gang in Atlanta, but they big enough to make people afraid. An' they got a mean streak. They may say brothers, but it ain't no brotherhood. Give 'em another couple years an' they'll fall apart, or get busted. Us normal folk, we jus' try an' keep our heads low an' go 'bout our lives. Poor Cory, he thought he had a big break. A way out. Now he's in a ditch somewhere, more'n likely."

"Well, if he's still alive, I'll find him," Sebastian said. No need to mention how he planned on doing that, including what Fester Jones had coming to him for sending Sebastian on a wild goose chase through Atlanta's most unsavory holes when that Southland Bastard probably knew exactly where Cory was. He should've paid closer attention to his coin.

"I sure hope you do," Pearl said, interrupting his train of thought. "Now, afore you start thinking 'bout leaving, you gonna explain what you was doin' back there?" She smiled at Sebastian's look of dismay. "No, I ain't forgot."

He chuckled ruefully, setting down his coke on the counter and facing Pearl. Usually he only spoke of his witchcraft with paying clients. But something about Pearl made him want her understanding, her acceptance. "I could tell you, I guess. But you won't believe me."

She cocked her head. "Try me."

He reached in his pocket and handed her one of his business cards. She took a moment to read it, eyebrows rising higher and higher, almost disappearing into her hairline. She gave him an incredulous look, and he could tell she was caught between laughing in disbelief and laughing at him for being serious. He was used to it. Sometimes the truth was stranger than fiction.

"You're a witch?" she asked, obviously unsure what to think.

"Yep. Curses and all."

She didn't laugh. Instead, she looked thoughtful. "But... curses, they don't squeak. Yore tryin' to make me think you're crazy, so's you don't have to explain. But I know what I heard back there."

"You're right, you caught me," Sebastian said, throwing up his hands in mock surrender. "I have a pet bat."

Pearl did laugh that time. "Really, now. Stop messin' with me."

"Okay, okay, I don't have a pet bat. But I *am* a witch. I know where to find backup if I need it." He gave her a roguish wink.

She still didn't look convinced. "Backup. You mean like ghosts or something?"

"Maybe. Sometimes." He shrugged. "But ghosts tend to be single-minded and motivated by a goal unique to why they stayed behind. They don't make good backup."

"So, what's the noise I heard?" she persisted, eyebrows raised.

Sebastian sighed. "A little friend of mine named Pip. Now, I don't want to be keeping you—"

"Wait, like, a fairy or something?" Pearl interrupted him.

Deciding to reward her open-minded persistence, he finally gave a real answer. "Pixie, actually. Suckers for hard liquor. They have an addiction problem, the little blighters. Easy to bribe in a pinch, you just have to follow through or they'll make your life hell."

"Oh," she said in a small voice. There was a long silence as she stared at her coke. "But..." she said after a moment, hesitating, "I thought witches used ghouls an' demons an' creepy critters like that?"

He shrugged again, picking up his coke for a drink. "They can. Some do. I don't." Not anymore, he added to himself. He'd learned his lessons the hard way.

"So, you gonna put a curse on Cory?" she asked, finally looking up at him, eyes searching.

Sebastian almost snorted his swig of coke up his nose at her question. Coughing, he put the coke down again and cleared his throat. "As satisfying as it would be to see him dance, no. I wouldn't curse a friend, even if he is a scumbag."

"Now, don't go talkin' 'bout him like that," Pearl scolded, looking relieved. "He got his problems, sure enough. But 'neath all that's a good heart."

"More likely, he just cleans up his act for a pretty lady," Sebastian said, winking.

At least the whole thing wasn't a bust, he thought, looking at Pearl. Maybe, someday, he could get to know her better. She seemed awfully nice to live in such a rundown place. Someday, he wanted to know her hopes and dreams, her plans for the future. Maybe he could help her get to wherever she hoped to go. Someday. But not today. Today he had a mission, and it involved quite a bit of butt-kicking.

"Thanks for the coke, Pearl, and the information. I stand by my original statement, that you're a deserving girl, not to mention pretty." He winked at her. "I'll try to keep Cory away from bars. Well, away from Atlanta in general if I can help it. If you never see him again, then I've done my job. But maybe I'll pop in sometime to say hello."

Pearl smiled and nodded. "You gonna pull a rabbit outta a hat for me someday?"

Pushing himself off the counter, he chuckled. "Now you're getting witches mixed up with magicians. If I need a rabbit I'll find a pet store. I can, however, bring you flowers." As he spoke, he leaned forward and produced a flower from behind Pearl's ear. Of course, it was only one of the plastic flowers from the vase on her table which he'd snagged using sleight of hand. But the trick put a smile on her face all the same.

"I'd like that," she said.

"So would I," Sebastian assured her. "So would I."

This time he kept the screen door open, waiting on the crumbling doorstep after giving Fester Jones' door a firm knock. When it finally cracked open, he abandoned all semblance of decorum and shoved his foot in the gap, getting enough leverage to force the door all the way open. Fester stumbled back, Sebastian's aggression taking him by surprise. Knowing he was in trouble, the scrawny man tried to scramble away, but Sebastian was quicker. Catching him with a solid cuff on the side of the head, he knocked the man off balance and got a firm grip on his collar, pushing him against the wall. Surprisingly, that was all he needed to thoroughly cow Fester, who now shook like a leaf, a mocking testament to the proud gang symbol tattooed on his wrist.

"So. Fester," Sebastian began, voice deceptively calm. "Tell me again how you haven't seen Cory in 'a spell.' Tell me again how you have no idea where he is or what's happened to him. Go on, tell me. I dare you."

"O—o—okay, okay!" the man stammered, eyes wide and fearful. "He—he's in a safe house. I can show you where on a m—map."

Sebastian's coin blazed hot in his pocket. "Liar. Try again." He put more pressure on the man's neck.

"Geeze, okay! S—stop it, will you?" Fester gasped, pushing feebly against Sebastian's grip. Sebastian let up a bit. "I ain't seen him in weeks. He—he got himself in trouble. Big trouble. Took off. There's some guys lookin' for him, probably got him by now. How 'bout I set up a meet, okay? You can ask them. They'll know where he is."

Stepping back, Sebastian let go and glared at Fester, trying to decide. The problem with a truth coin was that it didn't tell you *what* was a lie, just that there was one. It was a helpful trinket, but had its limits. This little weasel was mostly telling the truth, but the situation still smelled fishy. Yet the genuinely terrified look in his eyes when he mentioned "big trouble" made Sebastian's stomach tighten. What Cory had done to him was low. It hurt to be betrayed by someone he'd only tried to help. But addicts couldn't help themselves. He knew that. Cory needed help, and the only thing he would get on this track was a bullet to the head. If Sebastian could find out what was stolen, maybe he could make it right somehow, get these people off his friend's back. Maybe with the problem gone, Cory would be easier to find. Then all he had to do was get back his artifact, and check that sorry excuse for a human into rehab.

"Alright, set up a meet," he said.

Fester had given him directions to a run-down building in one of the more unsavory neighborhoods, saying someone would meet him there at 9:00 p.m., sharp. Well, someone met him all right. They jumped him the moment he walked in the door. Though half expected, it still took him by surprise. He could have fought back, but then he'd never find out what was going on and that would annoy him. Not to mention never finding the artifact. So he let them pull a bag over his head, tie his hands behind his back, and bundle him into what sounded like a van which screeched off into the night as soon as he was thrown inside.

Now he lay on the carpeted floor, wrinkling his nose at the stink of cigarette smoke and other less savory things strong enough to smell even through the bag. Listening to the engine hum, he wondered which body part they would threaten to break first, or if they'd just skip straight to a bullet in the head. Criminals were sadly predictable, especially those with so little self-respect as to wear their pants around their knees.

After five minutes, he got tired of lying on his side and rolled over to sit up. As soon as he raised his body, a foot shoved him back down. He sat up again, and the foot shoved him down a second time, more roughly.

"Keep your ass on the floor, or I'll put a bullet in it," said a voice he assumed belonged to the owner of the foot.

He chuckled. "Excellent suggestion, except that I *am* keeping my bottom firmly in contact with the floor already. It's my head you seem to have a problem with. And I suggest you come up with a more realistic threat, because you'd be an idiot to shoot me in a moving vehicle. The bullet could hit who knows what and kill us all. Then again," he mused, reconsidering, "you *are* an idiot, which means you'd probably be stupid enough to do it."

"Shut your face, freak, or I'll—" the voice began angrily.

"—you'll what? Oh please, do tell. Just make it good. If it involves a gun, I may die of boredom."

The thug's response was a kick to the ribs, driving all the breath out of Sebastian's body and making him curl to the side. As unwise as he knew it was to taunt his captors, he couldn't resist. He'd never been able to abide bullies, especially stupid ones.

"Oh, bravo. A really brilliant stroke," Sebastian coughed out as he tried to catch his breath. "I'm sure you're known by all your friends as the fiercest kicker in all of Southland.

Your mother would be so proud of you, attacking a bound man, lying helpless on the floor. It's such a brave step toward actually having a pair."

"Shut the fuck up!" the faceless thug growled, and Sebastian heard the rustling of his pant leg in time to roll away from the next kick.

"Give it a rest TJ, he's jus' messin' with you," a voice called from the front of the van, probably the driver.

"But this little—"

"Shut up, TJ. He'll get what's comin' to him," the driver said.

"Fine," the first thug grumbled, and Sebastian grinned beneath his bag. The next time he tried to sit up, no foot kicked him down, and he spent the rest of the trip leaning against the side of the van, counting.

When they arrived approximately fifteen minutes later, Sebastian calculated they were in the central or south central area of Atlanta. Knowing the area's reputation for drug trade, he was unhappy, but not surprised.

His captors pulled him roughly from the van, leading him blindly down a sidewalk and then into an alleyway between two buildings. He knew this from the echo of their footsteps bouncing off the surrounding terrain. He heard the scrape of a metal door being opened and was then shoved into a building that sounded empty and unfinished—echoes bouncing off concrete floor and walls sounded very different from echoes off a finished floor and drywall. The lights overhead buzzed like fluorescent lamps and he could make out the glow of their long shapes through the bag on his head. He was led through several rooms, some of them virtually empty and some occupied by men conversing in low voices, occasionally breaking out in nasty laughs as jokes were shot in his direction. Finally, they led him up a flight of stairs to a second story. He was sat roughly down in a wooden chair and tied to it. The men who led him up had a low conversation with someone across the room, and he also heard the sound of whimpering and the scraping of chairs. Then his captors traipsed back down the stairs, their footsteps echoing off the cement.

Cocking an ear, Sebastian grinned beneath the bag. At this point he was supposed to be frightened and intimidated, wondering what they would do to him. He could feel someone watching him from across the room.

"Look, could we just get on with it?" he asked the silent figure. "I'm on a tight schedule and wouldn't want to miss my appointment with the next gorilla who wants to threaten me."

There was no response, but after a few moments he heard footsteps approach. The bag was ripped off his head and he squinted in the fluorescent light. The man standing over him was tall and muscular, hard-faced and grim. Sebastian was surprised. He didn't look like your typical punk material, here to rough him up over some stolen money. This guy looked experienced. Probably the boss. What in the world had Cory done?

The man put a foot up on the seat of the chair, between Sebastian's legs, and leaned in, looming over him. "You got a schedule to keep, huh? Well, that's the least of your worries. Right now you should worry about whether I'm gonna blow your brains out."

Well, that was just peachy, Sebastian thought. Time to stall. "Obviously you want something, or else you'd have already done it," Sebastian replied, feigning boredom as he scanned the room. It was then that he spotted the source of the whimpering. Tied to a chair similar to his was Fester

Jones, face black and bloody from a beating. He avoided Sebastian's gaze, staring at the floor as he shook in fear.

Sebastian wasn't scared, exactly, but he did have a healthy respect for death threats. And it seemed the thug wasn't bluffing, because the bloodstains on the floor didn't all belong to Fester. There were too many and some were quite old. Time to tread lightly. "So, why don't you explain what's going on and I'll see how I can help."

"You can help by telling me where the hell that rat Cory is and what he did with my money," the boss yelled, getting right in Sebastian's face. His breath stank of stale cigarettes and vodka.

Making a face, Sebastian leaned away from the offending smell. "Now why in the world would I know that? Good grief, I came to *you* looking for him. He stole my stuff too. Though, judging by your operation," he peeked around the man's bulk and eyed the wads of cash and bags of white powder on the desk in the corner, "he probably took more from you than from me."

The man stood up, scowling, and glanced back and forth between his two captives, finally settling his glare on Fester. "What kind of story is this joker feeding me?" he asked, moving to loom menacingly over the man. "If this guy isn't for real, I'm gonna kill you both, you sorry, sniveling, piece of shit." He turned back to Sebastian. "He said you was Cory's contact. That you came to rat on him and get a reward. Well the reward is staying alive. Now stop playing games and start talking."

Sebastian sighed. He would have rubbed his temples if his hands hadn't been tied. Apparently, in some wild and unrealistic fantasy, Fester had imagined he would get a pat on the back for telling falsehoods and "handing" him in. By the look on Fester's bloody face, the man had realized the flaw in his plan.

"Obviously, there's been some kind of misunderstanding," Sebastian began, calmly, only to be cut off by a solid punch to the jaw that whipped his head painfully to the side.

"Yeah? Well 'obviously' you think I'm playing some sorta game," the boss said. "That scum stole from me and then had the balls to rat to the cops. He lost me a whole shipment and now the cops are breathing down my neck. I'm gonna find that little shit, cut off his balls and feed 'em to him. Now tell me where he is, or I'll find a better use for your hands than being attached to your body." He drew out a knife from his pocket and flicked it open. As he did, Sebastian saw the SLB tattoo on the inside of his wrist.

Ah. So that's what Cory had done. Well, points for ratting out this ugly excuse for a human, but that still left Sebastian bound to a chair, being threatened with dismemberment. It wasn't as bad as it sounded—he had a few tricks up his sleeve—but it was still pretty bad.

But just as he opened his mouth to speak—what, he had no idea, but something would come to him—there came a shout from downstairs.

"Hey boss! Big Cs on the phone for you, says it's important."

The boss snorted, flicking his knife closed again. "Looks like you two get a little time to get your story straight and save your sorry asses." He turned and descended the stairs, starting a muted conversation that Sebastian was utterly uninterested in.

Ignoring the sniveling Fester, Sebastian tested his bonds, making sure they gave when he pulled. Then he started whispering. "Elwa, Jastiri'un. I know you're still mad at me about last time, but I really need your help. I'll make it worth your time, I promise." He waited a few heartbeats, but there was no sound. "Come on, Jas. I know how much you love messing with people. I've got the perfect thing for you. I'll give—I'll *consider* giving you anything, just name your terms." He fell silent again, waiting with bated breath, heart pounding. In his desperate rush, he'd almost promised to give Jas anything. Accidental or not, if Jas had taken the deal, Sebastian would be bound to his promise.

Finally, there was a slight waver in the air in front of him, and a pixie appeared. But this was no normal pixie. Sebastian didn't know if he'd always been that way or had changed over time, but the creature he called Jas wasn't exactly corporeal. Fae, from what he understood, were purely magical beings given physical form. Jas loved waves of any kind. Radio, light, sound. He loved playing with them. Maybe he played with them so much, he became like them. In any case, he looked like a constantly shifting, dancing hologram. Sebastian didn't even know if Jas was a he. It was just the pronoun that seemed to fit him the best.

"Ah, there you are, I—" but he was interrupted by rapid squeaking. It wasn't really squeaking, just very fast, high-pitched talking. It took a lot of practice to understand. Practice that Sebastian had. He'd spent enough time in…well, he'd been around them enough to know.

"Okay, okay, I got it. A White Russian every night for a month," Sebastian said. Mixed drinks were as good as gold to pixies, who couldn't quite grasp the principles of mixology. They just knew mixed drinks were good and didn't come in a bottle. "Yeah, and no more comments about your taste in music. Sorry, I didn't know you were so touchy on the sub—" more squeaking "—right, sorry, when you said no more comments you meant no more comments. Do we have a deal?"

An affirmative squeak.

"Great, listen up. I need you to call every cop in the area to this building, now. Get on their radios, fake a dispatch call. Say there's armed men, money, and drugs, a gang called the Southland Brothers. Then, get the men downstairs fighting. I know you don't need any pointers on that," he winked at the hovering hologram, and it gave a squeaking laugh. "Don't let anyone leave until the cops get here, okay?"

Jas nodded and, with a crackling like radio static, disappeared. Sebastian hoped there were some cops close by. Things were about to get ugly, fast, and he wanted the authorities to catch these criminals at the scene—blood, money, drugs, and all.

He had finished talking with Jas none too soon, as the sound of booted footfalls drifted up the stairs. Soon the boss was back in front of his chair, smiling dangerously. He flicked out his knife again. "Now, where were we?"

Sebastian grinned. "I think we were discussing how proud your mother was when you won the dumbest man alive contest. It was really quite an achievement for you, considering."

"Why you little," The boss backhanded him, and Sebastian rolled with it, letting the force of the blow glance off his cheek. Looking back, he could see the fury in the man's eyes wasn't quite out of control. Well, he couldn't have that. Time to push more buttons.

"Your girlfriend must really love money, since there's nothing else attractive about a repulsive, spineless, moronic bully like you."

He almost didn't get to finish his insult before the man, face redder than a tomato, dropped his knife and grabbed him by the front of the shirt with both hands.

In a flash, Sebastian whipped his hands out from behind him where they'd been bound to the chair, grabbing the thug by the back of the neck as he head butted him solidly. He made sure to keep his chin tucked, striking the boss full in the face with the crown of his head. With a crunch, the man's nose broke, and he was out cold.

Pushing the unconscious, bleeding form off him and onto the floor, Sebastian stood. "You know," he said to empty air, "you really ought to hire men that tie better knots." That wasn't quite fair, since he technically couldn't be bound by human means anyway, thanks to another fae ability he'd picked up, but nobody needed to know that.

Cocking an ear, he thought he heard sirens in the distance, and he grinned. Good ol' Jas. Any minute now the chaos would start downstairs.

Sure enough, angry voices started floating up from below.

"What did you just say about my mother?"

"Hey, where'd my stack go, it was just here."

"You think *I* have a big mouth? It wasn't me who got himself thrown outa the club last week."

"If you call me that one more time, I swear I'll punch your face in."

The dull thump of fist hitting flesh was music to Sebastian's ears. Pretty soon people would start pulling guns. He'd seen it before. Jas loved sowing discord, more so than most pixies. So, being a manipulator of sound and light, he could easily make you hear and sometimes see whatever he wanted you to. He was a pixie alright; they lived for trouble. Yet, Sebastian felt no pity for these men. You reap what you sow.

Ignoring the sounds of escalating arguments downstairs, Sebastian moved to Fester's bound form and looked down at the trembling man. "Out of the goodness of my seriously pissed-off heart, I'm going to give a chance to redeem yourself." He leaned in. "Soon the cops will be here and this little gang will be toast. These low-life thugs hurt others and prey on weak, vulnerable people like my friend Cory. You strike me as a weak and vulnerable person yourself, and too much of a coward to get up to serious trouble. So, with your 'overlords' destined for lockup, I suggest you get someone to remove that tattoo. That is after, of course, you tell me where Cory is. *Capisce*?"

Fester nodded vigorously, looking like a bobble-head doll. "I—I'll tell you, just d—don't hurt me. I didn't wanna sell you out, h—honest. Cory saved my life, an' then he got himself in trouble, an' I wanted to help but I was sc—scared. I told him he couldn't stay with me 'cause the gang, they knew we was tight. B—but I didn't tell them nothin'. They've been leanin' on me real hard, said they was gonna gut me an' my girl if I didn't find Cory an' the money. I didn't know what to do. Thought if they got you, they'd leave me alone."

Standing up, Sebastian considered the man's words, surprised to discover he had a spine after all. "Well, congratulations for being slightly less of a coward than I first assumed." He leaned back down again, face stony. "But you still haven't answered my question."

"O—okay, okay," Fester said, shaking even harder. "He's d—down in Pitts. Said he knew a place where he could lay low. That's all I know, I swear."

"No name? No address?" Sebastian got out his coin, wrapping his fingers around its cool surface.

"N—no, I swear. All he said was Pitts, no details."

Sebastian put the coin back in his pocket. "Fine. It's a start."

Turning in a circle, he took quick stock of the room and his escape options. Through one of the windows, he could see the roof of a shed next to the building. If he could get the window open, he could drop down and make a run for it before the cops got there. No need for him to get mixed up in it all. He was just the messenger.

After precious seconds wasted wrestling with the rusted window latches, he finally got it open. Then, taking the knife from the unconscious gang leader, he cut Fester's bonds and hauled him to his feet by his shirt collar. He pointed out the window at the shed. "Jump."

Fester shrank back. "I—I don't like heights," he stammered.

"Would you rather stay here and explain to the cops your place in this illustrious gang?" Sebastian asked with raised eyebrows.

Vigorous head shake.

"Fine. Out you go then."

But once Fester had climbed up and was sitting on the sill, legs dangling out, his fear overcame his don't-get-arrested instinct. "I th—think I'll just stay here."

He tried to turn, but with a roll of the eyes Sebastian pushed him out the window. The man didn't even have time to scream before he hit the shed roof. He lay there a moment, stunned, but then the sound of sirens seemed to rouse him to action. He scrambled to the roof edge and clambered down a series of garbage cans set beside the shed wall, then took off into the night.

Well, there was his good deed of the day, Sebastian thought. Hopefully the man had enough sense to stay out of trouble after this. Sebastian straddled the sill himself and was preparing to drop down when his eyes fell on the stacks of money, drugs, and bottles of alcohol sitting on the desk.

He had a sudden, fierce urge to rip off the boss's shirt and make a few Molotov cocktails to chuck down the stairs at the fighting gang members below. But a fire might destroy evidence, and the police needed everything intact to press charges. With a sigh, he settled for stuffing wads of bills into a grocery bag lying on the table. After a moment's consideration, he added the boss's bottle of vodka. All that alcohol he'd promised to Jas wasn't going to be cheap. Then he headed back out the window.

He was just rounding the corner three blocks down when the cop cars screeched to a halt in front of the building. Turning away, a slow smile spread across his face. Not his usual gig, taking down gangs. He tended to stick to wealthy, superstitious clients who made petty, if well-paying, requests and lapped up his tricks and illusions like drug addicts. But not a bad day's work, considering. With a bounce in his step, he set off to find a taxi and retrieve his car. It looked like he would be taking a field trip to Pitts. But first, he had a delivery to make.

Sebastian stood in the shadows across the street from Pearl Harris's apartment complex. From his vantage point, he could see her apartment door in the glow of the security lights. There was no guarantee she would come straight home from the bar, but if he'd timed it right, she should be arriving just about now.

Sure enough, her figure appeared from the gloom, on foot, coming from the direction of the bar. She looked tired, her head drooping and feet dragging wearily. Watching her closely as she climbed the steps, he smiled when she stopped abruptly at the sight of a plastic grocery bag hanging from her door handle. With hesitant motions, she unhooked it and peered inside. Though he wasn't close enough to see her face, he saw the shock in her body language. She pulled out a piece of paper from the bag, stared at the words scribbled on it, then shook herself. Looking around for observers, she quickly slipped inside and shut the door.

Mission accomplished, Sebastian emerged from his hiding place and headed down the street to his car, already packed and ready for his trip to Pitts.

As he got in and turned the key, he couldn't stop smiling, picturing Pearl's face in his mind and imagining her expression while reading the note he'd left in the bag:

I'm out. Get yourself out too.
- Cory

Episode 2

Möbius Strip

Chapter 1

The Uses of Moldy Pizza

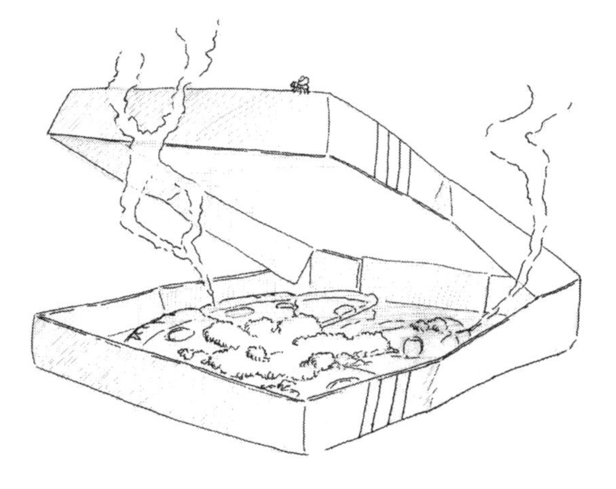

THOUGH NOT THE MOST AESTHETICALLY PLEASING OR COMFORTable place to read, the Basement was nonetheless Lily Singer's favorite. Hidden beneath the McCain Library of Agnes Scott College, this secret archive of wizardry and occult books lacked beams of sunlight to bask in, warm, fuzzy cats to pet, and a kitchen in which to make scones and tea—all delightful things, but distracting nonetheless. The Basement was silent as a grave and blessedly cool in the heat of the Atlanta summer. This peace and quiet, not to mention the plethora of magical wards, made it an ideal location for reading, studying, and practicing magic undisturbed.

She'd filled it with the comforts of home, of course. Being the archives manager of the library above and curator of the Basement's secrets, she had exclusive authority over its interior decoration. When her predecessor, Madam Barrington, had been its keeper, it had contained minimal decoration and only a few hardwood chairs—a reflection of her mentor's austere nature. Nothing had changed when Madam Barrington took on Lily as a student to teach her wizardry. That had been seven years ago during Lily's freshman year at Agnes Scott. It wasn't until her mentor had retired last year and left the Basement in her care that Lily took steps to make it a bit more welcoming.

First, she'd brightened the place up by renewing the light spells on the dozen dimmu-engraved glass balls hanging from the ceiling. No outlets or electrical wiring graced the Basement, since the whole thing had been magically created from a broom closet during the original 1936 construction of McCain Library—known then as the Carnegie Library. It had the advantage of being accessible only to wizards, and only to those who knew the access spell. Not that the Basement was much of a secret. Madam Barrington had said the Basement was frequented by numerous wizards at one point in time. But that must have been long ago, since Lily had only ever seen one other person there besides herself and her mentor. It seemed the Basement was protected by simple virtue of being forgotten.

With that in mind, she doubted anyone would ever see, or care, about her improvements, from hanging art on the walls to enchanting the dull ceiling to resemble the rib-vaulted heights of the library above. She'd added several small tables to display various magical knickknacks previously hidden away in drawers. There were items like a delicate antique engraver made entirely of spun lead except for its diamond tip, used to carve magical runes of power—dimmu runes—into any surface. Then there were the all-speak glasses, enchanted to translate any text into English for whoever was wearing them. Though quite useful, their creator must have had coprolalia, because the glasses had an annoying tendency to add random swear words to the translation.

As for other furniture, she'd left the large oak worktable, but the hardwood chairs had been relegated to stepping stools and replaced by several tastefully upholstered chintz chairs. How she'd managed to single-handedly maneuver those things down the archive steps, through the broom closet, and into the Basement, she had no idea. But she'd done it. Overall, the room's ambiance was much improved. It had become an island of peace in a world annoyingly full of people who, oddly enough, wanted to interact with her.

Thus it was quite shocking when her cell phone rang that Saturday afternoon. She was ensconced in a chintz chair, studying one of the books Sebastian had given her from Francis Jackson's estate. Not only was she underground—her cell barely got signal in the archive room next door—but the magical nature of the Basement completely scrambled electronic signals of any kind. After the first few seconds of shock wore off, she recognized the jaunty jingle of the 1960s theme song from *Bewitched.*

Lily rolled her eyes and sighed. If anyone could manage to call her underground in a signal blackout zone, it would be Sebastian. Leave it to him to disturb her peace. Being a witch, and a good one at that, he usually found a way. She considered not answering, but if he'd gone to this much trouble to call her, it was bound to be interesting if not important.

Setting down her book and picking up the phone, she put it to her ear. "This had better be good," she said, dispensing with pleasantries.

"It went through!" Sebastian exclaimed, his relieved voice distorted by static.

"How the heck are you calling me?" Lily demanded. "I don't get signal down here."

"Are you in the Basement? No wonder Jas had so much trouble finding you."

"What? Who's Jas?"

"Never mind, I don't have time."

"But—"

"Lily!" Sebastian yelled, startling her into affronted silence. After a hesitation, he continued, apologetic, "I'm sorry, but this is urgent and I don't have much time. I need you to do exactly as I say. Lives depend on it."

"Okay," she said, dubious but giving him the benefit of the doubt.

"I need you to meet me at 717 Eighth Street in Pitts at exactly, uhhh," he paused, "5:23 p.m. today. Exactly. And you need to stand on the curb, four steps away from the lamp pole."

"What?" Lily was thoroughly confused.

"No time to explain," Sebastian said, tone urgent. "Just promise you'll be there."

"I—" she began, but he interrupted.

"Oh, and you need to bring a box of old pizza from my house. The kitchen window is loose, you can get in that way."

"I'm not going into that dump," she protested.

"You…have to!" Sebastian's voice started breaking up even more, half his words lost in the crackle. "I…it…. crazy…have…promise…be…5:23…pizza…promise me!"

"Okay, okay, I'll—" Lily started, but the call had already dropped. She looked at the phone in consternation, exceedingly annoyed.

"Humph. A pox on you, Sebastian," she grumbled, unfolding from her curled-up position in the chintz chair and reaching for a pencil to write down his crazy request before she forgot the details. She'd planned to spend the entire day in quiet solitude, just her and her books. So much for that.

As she gathered her things, she considered—not for the first time—blocking Sebastian on her phone. But she had a soft spot for adventure, and, no matter how annoying he was, that charming ne'er-do-well always seemed to find it. Besides, who else would be there to get him out of trouble if not her?

Looking around, Lily ensured she'd left everything in order, then headed for the door. Before she exited, she said a word to dim the lights and another to activate the passive spell which would alert her if anyone tried to force entry. There was no door to lock—it was, after all, a public collection of sorts. Instead, spells much older and stronger than she could ever cast protected the items within, preventing their removal, destruction, or alteration by anyone but her, the gatekeeper. Ensuring the room was properly warded, she left, emerging into the archives broom closet. After a quick peek to check that the archives were empty, she slipped out of the closet and shut the door behind her. Only Penny, her archives assistant, had access to the archives room besides her, but it was always safer to check. Everyone knew Lily spent hours in the archives conducting esoteric research, so no questions were asked and everyone remained blithely unaware of the wizard's library beneath their feet.

With a sigh, she turned off the lights, locked the archives door behind her, and trudged up the steps to the main library and her office. Time to find out where the heck Pitts was.

★ ★ ★ ★

Lily glanced at her watch. It was 5:20 pm. She stood exactly where Sebastian had asked and, distastefully holding the box of moldy pizza as far away from her as possible, gazed around at the deserted street. Pitts, as it turned out, was a tiny town in south Georgia, about a two-hour drive from Atlanta. According to the latest census, it had a whopping population of 302 people.

The odd thing was that not a single soul was visible. Even in a town this small there should have been *someone* on the main thoroughfare, but it was deserted. Several pickups were parked down the street, and the single strip of small-town stores looked as lived-in as possible in a place this remote. The 5 and Dime general store had an "OPEN" sign hanging inside its glass door, and the antique shop across the street had a running electric fan which rotated slowly back and forth, cooling a nonexistent customer base. It was as if everyone had disappeared moments before, leaving the street exactly as it was.

She shivered, standing just inside a shadow cast by the two-story brick building between her and the hot Georgia sun. This town creeped her out. She glanced at her watch again. 5:23 had arrived, but Sebastian had not. That was odd, given how insistent he'd been on the exactness of the time. She was going to kill him for dragging her all the way out here without telling her why if, on top of that, he was late.

A minute passed, then another. At 5:25, Lily was ready to give up in disgust. Instead of leaving, she decided to head over to the general store and see if anyone was around who could explain what the heck was going on. As she stepped out onto the street, she felt a sudden tug of magic and—

HOOOONK!!!

The deafening blare of a car horn assaulted her ears as a hand came out of nowhere and jerked her back onto the curb. In that split second, the whole street was transformed. People appeared where there had been none, and cars filled a previously empty street. The mysterious hand had pulled her back just in time to avoid getting hit by a dusty pickup truck that had seen better days, yet still moved at a respectable clip.

"I said to meet me on the *curb*, not in the street! What are you trying to do, get yourself killed?" Sebastian's voice came from behind her, and strong hands turned her shocked body around so he could look her up and down. His drawn, tired face showed worry as he took the pizza box from her hands and checked her for injury.

Lily shrugged off his hands, switching to no-nonsense "research" mode to hide her tremor and racing pulse. "I'm fine. Where am I and what just happened? This place was deserted a second ago. What's going on?"

Sebastian grinned, a bit of his normal self showing through. "Well, I *was* being bored to death, but now that you're here the real party can get started." He gave her a slap on the back and turned her with a flourish to begin guiding her down the street toward the outskirts of town.

Lily planted her feet and crossed her arms. "I'm not going anywhere until you tell me what's going on. You claimed lives were at stake. Did you just mean your own? You're either up to something questionable, or you've gotten yourself in a pickle. What did you do this time?"

"It's more along the lines of what I *didn't* do, actually." Sebastian sighed. "Can't I tell you on the way? We're a bit short on time here."

She glared at him for a moment, then relented. "Fine. But where are we going? I need to get some things from my car."

Pulling her along, Sebastian shook his head sadly. "Trust me, you're not going to see that car again until we fix this mess. Just come with me, I'll explain while we walk."

Feeling disoriented, Lily looked up the street to where she'd parked her car not five minutes ago. It was gone. She stared at the empty spot, unable to believe her eyes, only moving when Sebastian gently tugged on her arm to pull her down the street. She stayed on the opposite side of him from the box of molding pizza he held, trying to wrap her mind around what was going on. Waiting until they'd left the main part of town and no pedestrians were visible, she cleared her throat significantly, nudging her friend when he didn't respond.

"Huh?" Sebastian seemed to have been lost in thought.

"You start talking or I stop walking," Lily reminded him.

"Ah, yes. Well…it's a rather long story," he muttered, looking away.

"Then summarize," she insisted.

He chuckled ruefully. "Okay, if that's the way you want it, then here you go. A magical artifact I had in my possession, eh…went astray, ended up here, and is now being used to loop time into a never-ending day."

Lily stopped walking and stared at him, shocked all over again. It wasn't just the situation that upset her, but more so the audacity with which Sebastian blithely involved her in his self-made problems without asking permission first. It was exceedingly rude.

"Oh, yeah, and we're stuck here until we find it and stop it. I forgot that part," he added, giving her an apologetic shrug.

"Are you *absolutely* certain?" Lily asked, very slowly, very dangerously. "Because if this is a joke…" she let her words trail off, her implied threat all too obvious.

"The only certain things in life are death and taxes," Sebastian quipped, then paused. "Well, and gravity…and Murphy's law…" he caught her look and, no doubt recognizing the building thundercloud of fury, hurried on. "Yes, I'm certain. And might I point out that if you kill me now you'll never get out of here alive?"

Lily glared daggers at him, considering what curses would still leave him able to walk and talk, at least long enough to unravel this mess. As he withered under her gaze, however, she caught a glimpse of the worry hidden under his flippant bravado. He was in a mess, knew it, and needed her help. So she took a deep breath, reminded herself that curses would not help the situation, and began walking again. He fell into step beside her.

"Alright," she said, resigned, "start from the beginning. I want details. And if we ever get out of this, you owe me. Big."

Sebastian nodded glumly. Lily suspected he was remembering the last time he'd owed her and she'd called him on it. Well aware of his aversion to physical labor, she'd made him move heavy books. A lot of them. He'd complained, quite loudly, that he was allergic to "book dust." She'd made him do it anyway.

"So," Sebastian began, "I had this artifact—"

"And where did you get it?" Lily interrupted.

"Well, I 'acquired' it from my brother," he said evasively.

"Really? I didn't know you had a brother." Her interest was piqued. They rarely discussed personal matters. It was easier to keep things on a professional—well, a working-together level—that way. But she'd always been curious.

"Yes," Sebastian said, a note of distaste creeping into his voice. "Older by four years. Always the perfect son. Always Mother and Father's favorite."

Lily raised an eyebrow, unable to pass by such a convenient opportunity to poke at Sebastian's egotism. "A bit jealous, are you?"

Sebastian snorted. "He's a stuck-up prig."

"Not like anyone I know," she muttered.

"Hey," he said, feigning hurt. "I am not stuck up. I just have style."

That made Lily laugh.

Sebastian continued. "He always had to do everything just right, be the perfect student, get all the praise. Now he runs some big company or other, making lots of money and charming everybody into thinking he's a perfect person. But I know better."

Lily decided not to pursue that line of questioning. Sebastian's resentful look was foreboding, and she'd never been good at personal matters anyway.

"Okay, so you 'acquired' it from your brother," she prompted.

Sebastian grinned. "You could say that. I couldn't stand his Mr. Perfect act anymore, so I took it to prove he's not as good as he thinks he is."

That brought a disapproving frown to Lily's face. "Stealing is wrong, even from your own brother."

"Well, I wasn't planning on keeping it, so it's more like borrowing. I was going to wait a while, then show him he'd been missing it the whole time and give it back."

"What? Has he not noticed you took it yet?" she asked. "Isn't he a wizard?"

Sebastian threw back his head and laughed. "Of course he is. I told you, he's the perfect one. But he doesn't use magic. My family was not, ah…a normal wizard family. Had some pretty weird ideas about magic. Power corrupts, magic is power, therefore…you get the picture. As for the artifact, he just stuffed it in a safe and forgot about it."

"So where did your brother get this artifact?" Lily asked. "And you still haven't told me what it is."

Sebastian waved a hand. "I'll get there. It was willed to him by our parents."

"Oh? Then how did he get it if…I mean…your parents…" she faltered, suddenly realizing the implication of his words.

Sebastian shrugged in an attempt to seem casual, but the sudden stiffness in his shoulders and discomfort in his voice was obvious. "They died when I was a teenager. Car wreck. Freddie was busy getting his degree, so Aunt Barrington took me in till I was legal."

Lily looked at the ground, embarrassed. "I'm sorry…I didn't know." She felt terrible. It was hard, not knowing who her father was, but at least she had parents. Sebastian had no one. She felt a little closer to him in that moment, both of them being estranged from their families, though for different reasons. She wondered how deep he'd had to bury that loss to act as cheerful and carefree as he did all the time.

They walked in silence for a while.

"So, if Madam B. helped raise you, why did she disown you?" Lily couldn't help asking.

Sebastian snorted. "That old bat has a superiority complex a mile wide. Freddie was perfect. He was a wizard, even if he did have silly notions about magic. But me, I had nothing. Since I couldn't be who she wanted me to be, I decided to be someone *I* wanted to be, someone useful. So I studied witchcraft on my own. It's all about give and take, favors, who and what you know. I get more respect from the beings I deal with than I ever got from her."

"Oh," Lily said, her voice small. So, Sebastian was part of a dying wizard line. That explained why Madam Barrington had always refused to discuss it. She itched to know more, but they were getting distracted from the point.

"So...Freddie was willed the artifact, and you took it. What happened next?"

"Nothing, really," Sebastian said, a bit embarrassed. "I mean, I fiddled with it some to see if I could get it to work. I thought maybe...well, if it worked, then maybe...the night my parents died...but I guess it only works for wizards. It's supposed to be this ancient time-control device. My family has kept it for generations, to keep it safe from people who would abuse it. At least that's what Father said. The whole idea is pretty silly if you ask me. If it's so dangerous, why not destroy it? I guess I never took him seriously."

He grew quiet, and Lily gave him space. The sidewalk they'd been on ended and they switched to walking on the shoulder of the road to avoid wading through knee-high grass. The air thrummed with the buzz of grasshoppers in the fields to either side, and the afternoon sun beat down on them, causing sweat to bead on her forehead.

"Anyway," Sebastian finally continued, "when they died, it passed to Freddie. It came with a letter that carried on and on about the dangers of magic, and how we had to guard the family's heritage without getting involved in it."

"Sounds like my Mom," Lily muttered, "though she didn't even give me the courtesy of a choice. She just cut me off from my past."

Sebastian shot her a sympathetic look. "I'm sure she meant it for the best. I'm no expert, but, from what I've picked up, wizard families have their fair share of crazies. Using magic can be dangerous."

Lily snorted, thinking of Annabelle, but didn't continue the topic. "So, how did the artifact end up here?"

A scowl appeared on Sebastian's face, and he kicked a rock on the road in an irritated gesture. It skittered off into the grass. "It's here because of a sorry thief named Cory. We were friends in high school. He's a decent enough guy, at least he used to be. But after high school he got addicted to gambling and wracked up a lot of debt. I tried to help him out. Well, more like I dragged him out of bars and kept bigger guys from beating the snot out of him. A couple weeks back—well, it could've been longer, this place messes with my sense of time—he showed up on my doorstep, plastered, and I took him in for the night. I'd planned to give him a bit of money and send him on his way the next day. But the scumbag was faking it and robbed me blind in the night. He made off with everything he could carry, including the artifact. He probably thought it looked valuable enough to pawn.

"I've been searching for him since, only recently gotten a lead on him. He's been hiding out in Pitts the whole time, that's why I couldn't find him in Atlanta. Well, that and the little time-looping fiasco you're here to help me fix. I got pulled in by accident, and once I was inside I couldn't get out. Plus, I didn't have the tools I needed to track him down."

Sebastian jiggled the pizza box significantly, and a wave of moldy pizza smell, magnified by the hot sun, wafted in Lily's direction. She coughed and moved upwind.

"Why the heck do you need nasty pizza to track down a thief?"

"You'll see," Sebastian said, grinning once more, probably in a better mood now that he was close to finding his quarry.

Lily wasn't done yet, however. "So what *is* this artifact? Are you sure it's what's causing all this?"

He shrugged. "I've no idea whether it can do diddly-squat, but what else could be to blame? You think there's a wizard running around casting time-looping spells?"

"No." Lily shook her head. "To even try would be insane."

"I thought all wizards were insane." Sebastian grinned.

She ignored his jibe. "What does it look like?"

"Well, it's a round cylinder about as long as my hand and wide as a silver dollar. It's made up of rotating dials, kind of like you see on a combination lock. The dials are all inscribed with tiny symbols, like the kind you use. I don't know what it's made of, but it feels like clay."

"Hmm…I guess it could be genuine," Lily mused. "What's its history?"

"Darned if I know. Father only mentioned it once, before Freddie left for college. That was before they…well you know. He called it a lu…luglam…lugnam—"

"*Lugal-nam*?" Lily asked, feeling a twinge of foreboding as she spoke the words. She'd heard them somewhere before, possibly even read them in her eduba. Unfortunately, she'd left her carpetbag full of supplies—including the eduba—in her car, not anticipating being stuck in a time loop.

"Yeah! That was it," Sebastian said. "I was, er, eavesdropping and heard him explaining how it would one day be Freddie's duty to keep it safe, make sure no one ever used it."

"So much for that," Lily said, rolling her eyes.

"Hey!" Sebastian protested, "I kept it secret and safe. It's not my fault I got robbed."

She snorted. "Like you robbed Freddie? At least *he* kept it locked up. Where did you keep it, in your sock drawer?"

"Well..." he scuffed the ground with his foot.

"You kept it in your sock drawer?" Lily asked, incredulous. "I was joking! Of all the idiotic, infantile—"

"Okay, okay!" Sebastian cut her off. "I messed up, I get it. Now will you please just help me find it and fix this mess?"

She heaved a great sigh. Sometimes Sebastian drove her to the edge of sanity. She wasn't sure yet, but, if this device was what she thought it was, they were in bigger trouble than even she had feared.

"It's not like I have a choice, at this point," she said, motioning to the fields and buzzing insects around her. "But why haven't you tried leaving? Where's your car? More important, where's mine?"

"Not here anymore. It's back in real time, whereas we're stuck in a time loop. And I *have* tried leaving. No matter how far I walk, I always end up back where I started. No idea how it works. I never turn around or reach a wall. It's like one of those silly strips of paper you twist and tape together, what are they called?"

"A Möbius strip?" Lily asked.

"Yeah, one of those. By my calculations, I've been here a week, real-time, trying to figure this out. It's pretty annoying living the same span of time over and over."

Lily's head felt fit to burst, trying to wrap her mind around the situation and Sebastian's words. The heat didn't help. Despite growing up in the Alabama backwaters, she'd never adapted to the heat and humidity. She preferred the cool, indoor refuge of her library, along with the relaxing solitude it offered.

"Alright, so let's say your theory is correct. Why isn't there a panic? Why isn't everybody running around, trying to escape?"

"Probably because no one here is any the wiser. It must be part of whatever magic is controlling this train wreck."

"What do you mean?" Lily asked, confused.

"I made a bargain with a fae once," he said, nonchalant. "She made it so magic can't mess with my head. If I remember the loop but no one else does, it must be magic causing them to forget."

"Is that so?" she asked, incredulous. According to legend, fae could see through illusions and were immune to things like glamour and mind control. But even *if* they were still around and *if* the legends were true, what would convince one to share such power, and with a mere human, no less?

"So what did you trade for it?" Lily joked, "a bit of your soul?"

"Are you crazy?" Sebastian sounded genuinely shocked. "People don't know enough about their souls to understand what pieces to trade. If you just say 'take a piece of my soul,' willy-nilly, they'll take the most important part."

She opened her mouth to argue, then closed it again, noticing as she did how deftly he'd avoided answering her question. How Sebastian remembered the time loop was, at the moment, moot. Right now she needed to focus on stopping it. There would be time to question his tall tales later.

"So what's the plan?" she asked wearily, wiping her sweaty forehead on her t-shirt sleeve.

"Well, now that I have this," he held up the pizza box, "we can find Cory. Once we find Cory and figure out what he did with the lugalana…the luglanana…oh forget it, the artifact, we can get our hands on it, and stop whoever keeps restarting the loop."

"Remind me again, how is moldy pizza going to help us find Cory?"

"Ah, an excellent question. Watch, and prepare to be impressed." Sebastian winked at her, veering off the road toward a nearby copse of trees. Lily eyed the tall grass with distaste, knowing well that chiggers and ticks hid therein. At least she'd had enough foresight to wear jeans and tennis shoes. She'd learned the hard way that her normal attire of heels, pencil skirt, and blouse were woefully inadequate when involved in one of Sebastian's adventures. With a sigh, she plunged into the grass after her intrepid friend.

Sebastian led her to a small spring which bubbled out of the ground within the group of trees. Its tiny flow created a soggy band of turf which meandered out into the field. Verdant weeds sprouted from the almost mini-swamp, and the humid air was ripe with the smell of mud and decaying vegetation.

"Perfect! This is just the spot," Sebastian said, looking around in satisfaction while Lily tried to find somewhere dry to stand.

"Now what?" she asked, having failed to find said dry spot and resigned herself to muddy sneakers.

"Now you sit back and watch a master at work," Sebastian said, twirling the box of pizza with a dramatic flourish. He opened the top and started waving it about, no doubt in an effort to distribute its smell over the surrounding grasses. Lily wrinkled her nose and squished away to stand upwind of his flailing display.

"Elwa Grimoli'un," he said to empty air, startling Lily with his use of some sort of foreign language. Not Enkinim, for sure. Another question to add to her list. "Come out, come out, you old coot," he continued in a conversational tone, "I know you're around somewhere. You can smell my aged pizza a realm away. Show your ugly face."

He continued this for another minute, and Lily wondered if he'd cracked in the heat. But then the grass around them started rustling, as if disturbed by a raccoon-sized animal. A line of swishing grass circled them, moving quickly. Nervous, Lily inched closer to Sebastian, bad smell forgotten. But before she had a chance to consider what spell to ready in case they were attacked, a gray, muddy ball of flesh leapt out of the weeds, aiming right for Sebastian's box of pizza.

Sebastian must have been expecting it, because he jerked the box up deftly, and the little muddy thing disappeared back into the grass.

"Ah ah ah!" he said. "You know the rules, you cretin. A service for a service. Don't be shy, the good-looking wizard is with me."

Lily glared at him and so missed seeing the whatever-it-was emerge from the grass. Thus, when she looked back down, she screamed and stumbled back in shock at finding it at her feet, sniffing her shoes.

"What in the—"

"Calm down, Lil, he's harmless. He doesn't eat shoes, or girls, for that matter. Some do, mind you. But he doesn't. Grimmold, meet Lily. Lily, Grimmold. We go way back, me and ol' Grim. Don't we, buddy?"

It...he...the thing ignored Sebastian, staring up at her with beady little eyes, its squashed-in face an ugly mass of wrinkles and mud. Then it scampered away, moving incredibly fast for such a squat, round thing, and clambered up a tree to perch on a limb, now eye-to-eye with Sebastian. She stared, needing to look away and look back in an attempt to focus because there was shimmering around the creature that made it hard to discern his exact features. They shifted, as if flickering between two versions of himself.

"Humph. She smell bad," it croaked.

"Excuse me? *I* smell bad?" Lily was outraged.

Sebastian laughed. "Don't get your knickers in a knot. He has a nose like a bloodhound on steroids, and he's highly allergic to soap or cleaning fluid of any kind. He probably smells whatever soap you used to shower this morning."

She crossed her arms, still miffed. "What is it…he?"

The creature glowered at her as Sebastian replied. "He's a mold fae. They eat decaying things, and Grimmold has quite a taste for moldy pizza. Like all fae, he has a…unique way of getting around, and with his nose he's absolutely fantastic at finding things. So, I bring him specially-aged pizza, and he finds what I want found. Why do you think I have all those pizza boxes around all the time?"

Lily stared in amazement at the creature. Here, right in front of her, was a real, live fae. She'd read about them. She'd known they existed, in theory. But she'd never really believed it, or imagined meeting one. And in Pitts, Georgia, no less.

"How did…where did…how long have you known?" Lily stammered.

"About what, the fae? Pish, I may not be a wizard, but I'm not exactly a mundane, either. My parents didn't want us involved in their world, your world. But they couldn't stop me. I've had, ah…dealings with the fae. They gave me this." He indicated the triangular stone around his neck that Lily had always wondered about.

"What is it?" she asked.

"It's a seeing stone, the only way non-fae can see through fae glamour. Here, take a look."

He took the stone from around his neck and handed it to her. Holding it up to her eye, she peered through the hole in the center at the mold fae. She wasn't sure what she should be seeing, because now he looked almost exactly the same, except without the shimmering. Strangely, however, when she pulled the stone away, everything stayed the same. The shimmering was gone. She handed it back to Sebastian.

"I don't know if it worked. He looks the same, just without the shimmering."

Sebastian laughed. "Well, mold fae aren't very self-conscious about their looks. They're ugly and don't care one bit. So they don't really use glamour except to hide. The shimmering, though…" He trailed off, looking at her strangely.

"Look, we can puzzle over fae later. Right now we have a job to do."

"Right, yeah. A job," he said slowly, mind obviously elsewhere.

"Me leaving," Grimmold grunted from his branch, turning to climb down the tree. He must have been as tired of waiting as Lily was.

"No, no! Hold up, now. I've got something for you."

He took a piece of pizza out of the box and threw it at the fae. In a flash, the creature reached out with arms as long as its body and snatched the piece out of the air, shoving it into his wide mouth. As the fae chewed, Lily stared at Sebastian in confusion. When he threw the pizza, she thought she'd caught a glimpse of a symbol on his hand out of the corner of her eye. Yet when she looked straight at him, it was gone. She looked away, to see if it became visible to indirect sight, but all she could see was that strange shimmering again out of the corner of her eye.

"A gift," Sebastian was saying, oblivious of Lily's stare as he focused on Grimmold, "to apologize for the soap. She didn't know."

Grimmold grunted in laughter, licking his fingers one by one. "Pizza good. What you need? Me want more."

"Ah yes, well," Sebastian juggled the pizza box to his other hand, reaching into his back pocket and pulling forth a ziplock bag containing a much-wrinkled sock. He extracted the sock and dangled it in front of Grimmold's nose.

"This belongs to a human named Cory. I think he's here, in the time bubble or whatever it is, and I need to find him. Can you do it? I wasn't sure if this whole timey-wimey thing would throw you for a loop, no pun intended." He winked at Lily, who suppressed a smile.

Grimmold clutched the sock to his squashed nose, breathing deeply and leaving muddy handprints on the already less-than-clean sock.

"Hm. Foot mold. Me like."

The fae lowered the sock and started smelling the wind, turning his head this way and that.

"Can you do it?" Sebastian asked again.

Grimmold nodded. "What me get?" He eyed the pizza box greedily.

"If you will lead us *safely* to Cory, you get half now, half when we arrive."

"Deal. Gimme," Grimmold said, not one to waste words as he held his hands outstretched toward the pungent box.

Sebastian chuckled, opening the box once more and feeding half the remaining slices to his grimy mold-fae-hound, one by one.

"I always have to remember to say 'safely'," Sebastian muttered to Lily out of the side of his mouth as Grimmold stuffed his face. "Ask me someday about the time I forgot and almost got stuck in between worlds."

Lily just stood there, fascinated, still trying to process the scene. Despite her theoretical knowledge of the Source—what society today called magic—and the beings besides humans connected to it, meeting one in person was nonetheless overwhelming. It was the first time she'd ever come face to face with a fae, and her fingers itched for a pencil and her eduba so she could take a magical snapshot and notate her observations. If only she had time to study it, to take a closer look. Well, not too close. He was *very* muddy.

Heedless of her fascination, Grimmold made quick work of the pizza. Once he'd eaten the last of his allotted amount, Sebastian firmly closed the box lid and put his free hand on his hip. "Alright, Grimmold, lead the way."

With one last, longing look at the box in Sebastian's hand, Grimmold swung off the limb, landing with a plop in the muddy spring and splashing Lily's pant legs with muck.

"Hey!" she exclaimed, backing up hastily.

But the creature had already started off into the grass, invisible but for the line of waving stalks that marked his passage.

"Don't dally, or we'll lose him," Sebastian said, moving quickly to follow the fae.

Lily glared balefully at her friend's retreating form as he waded heedlessly through the tick-infested grass. Gritting her teeth, she started off after the muddy fae and crazy witch, trying to think of the most unpleasant, arduous favor possible to inflict on Sebastian after this was all over.

Chapter 2

Somewhere In-Between

GRIMMOLD LED THEM BACK IN THE GENERAL DIRECTION OF TOWN, but at an angle headed more south than east. After traipsing through two fields, over a fence, and across a stream, Lily was relieved to spot a country road. It paralleled the path Sebastian was currently blazing through waist-high weeds, hot on the heels of his impromptu bloodhound. Veering to the right, she made a beeline for it. It wasn't that she couldn't manage the outdoors; she just saw no reason to endure its discomfort unnecessarily.

Emerging into the open with a sigh of relief, she took a moment to brush off the stickers and various bits of nature clinging to her jeans before trotting to catch up with Sebastian. He still forged onward, about twenty yards to her left, following the waving line of weeds that indicated Grimmold's progress.

Looking past Sebastian to the northeast, she spotted the tops of the buildings that passed for downtown Pitts in the distance. The road in front of her ran straight, and far ahead she could see houses on either side. She wondered how far the time loop's physical boundary extended. A mile? Two?

"You know, you could walk on the road," Lily called out to Sebastian.

"Tell that to Grimmold," Sebastian called back, struggling to untangle himself from a thorn bush with one hand while balancing his pizza box in the other. He aimed a few choice words at the line of rustling weeds that pulled ahead, ignoring his plight. Eventually, he extracted himself and ran to catch up.

"This little git doesn't like being out in the open," he said in way of explanation. "That, and he enjoys making me suffer."

She wasn't sure, but Lily could have sworn she heard a grunting snicker come from the weeds ahead of Sebastian.

It took another five minutes to reach the houses. They each sat a little back from the road, their yards' grass ranging from well kept to so high that the yards were indistinguishable from the fields behind them. A substantial ditch ran alongside the road, full of nettles and stickers. To this jungle of weeds Grimmold headed. Now that the fae was close to the road, Sebastian, grumbling under his breath, gave up following him and joined Lily.

"Not so keen on this whole 'let's follow the fae' thing anymore, are you?" Lily grinned.

"He's led me through worse," Sebastian replied, vigorously dusting himself off, though that hardly made a dent in the forest of stickers that covered him from the waist down.

He finally shrugged and gave up, keeping pace with Grimmold to his left and Lily to his right.

After several more minutes, the fae stopped at the driveway of a particularly run-down house whose yard was of the "indistinguishable" variety. Poking his head out from between the weeds, he pointed behind himself at the house.

"He there."

"Are you sure?" Sebastian asked, suspicious.

Grimmold scowled, holding out his hand for payment. "Never wrong. Gimme."

Sebastian sighed but did as requested, dumping the remaining pieces of pizza on the ground in front of the muddy fae and chucking the empty box in one of several overflowing garbage cans by the driveway. Lily's eyes followed Sebastian's movements, and when she looked back down both the fae and the pizza were gone.

"Don't worry," Sebastian said. "He never *is* wrong, at least not as long as I've known him. If he says Cory is here, the scumbag is here. Come on."

Sebastian led the two of them down the gravel drive and onto the rickety wood porch. He pulled back the sagging screen door and knocked firmly, then hastily grabbed Lily by the shoulders and positioned her squarely in front of the door before slipping to the side. He placed his back to the wall, where someone opening the door wouldn't see him.

Lily opened her mouth to protest but closed it again at his frantic shushing motion. She rolled her eyes and waited, deciding he didn't want to be seen in case Cory was the one to answer the door.

Nothing happened, however, and Lily wondered if anyone was home. An old car sat out front, but it looked so decrepit she couldn't decide if it was usable or not. She tried knocking again, knuckles brushing off bits of flaking brown paint from the door. The paint chips fell to the porch, joining the general population of dirt that resided there.

Finally, she heard footsteps and muffled voices. A woman of indeterminate age threw open the door, looking like she'd just woken up. Though probably only thirty or forty, her wrinkled skin, sunken face, and stringy hair made her look more like fifty. She wore a ratty t-shirt, boxer shorts, and dirty house shoes.

"Waddaya want?" she asked, speech slurred.

Lily stood, lips parted, suddenly unsure what to say.

As if on cue, Sebastian bobbed in from the side, interrupting before her incoherent stammers had a chance to leave her lips.

"Ah! My good woman, so nice to meet you. My name is Oscar, and I'm an old friend of Cory's. I was passing through and thought I'd pop in and say hello. Is he here?"

The woman stared at him, momentarily stunned, perhaps by his irrepressibly chipper manner.

Lily hid a grin, amused by the sometimes pompous mannerisms Sebastian adopted when he was trying too hard to be charming.

"Yeah, he's here," the woman said finally. "But he's sleepin'."

"I'm sorry to come at a bad time, but I *am* just passing through, and I can't stay long. I know he would be quite disappointed to miss me. Could we come in for a moment?"

The woman thought about that, then shrugged, obviously not caring much either way. She gestured for them to enter, then disappeared back into the darkness of the house, yelling as she did.

"Cory! Get yer butt outa bed! Guy named Oscar's here, says he's yer pal."

Following on the woman's heels, Sebastian entered first with Lily bringing up the reluctant rear. Wrinkling her nose at the overwhelming smell of cigarette smoke, she stepped into the dimness. She was just in time to see the woman disappear into what was presumably her bedroom and shut the door. Lily frowned in disapproval at the lack of hospitality—the woman hadn't so much as offered them a seat or a drink.

Sebastian headed straight for the half-open door further down the hall from which muttered curses emanated. He slipped in without knocking, and soon the muttered curses became much louder and were accompanied by sounds of a scuffle. By the time Lily cautiously poked her head into the room, Sebastian had Cory pinned to the bed, one knee on the disheveled man's chest and one hand circling his throat. The other hand was in his pocket, of all places, but Lily was too distracted to wonder why.

Cory looked both shocked and pitiful, and he must have been suffering from a massive hangover by the universal oh-god-kill-me-now-just-please-stop-that-racket-look on his face. Though no less slender than Sebastian, and not much shorter, his flabby limbs were no match for his opponent's wiry strength.

"Don't hurt him," Lily hissed, though even if she'd yelled, the woman in the next room probably wouldn't have cared.

"He's fine," Sebastian said, unconcerned. Then he glanced at his watch and cursed. "We don't have much time. Let me do the talking."

"Wha—"

But Sebastian was already interrogating Cory.

"Where's all my stuff?"

Cory gurgled, and Sebastian eased his grip slightly. Panting, eyes darting back and forth, Cory spoke in a pleading voice, "I don't have it, man. I sold it already."

Sebastian seemed to think about this a moment, looking into the frightened man's eyes before nodding, as if he'd just decided to believe him. "Then where's my money?" Her friend's expression remained hard and his words harsh.

Cory gulped. "Gimme a break, Seb. I owed money to some really bad dudes. All that went straight to them. If you'd've just given me a little help, I wouldn't've had to—"

"Don't even start," Sebastian cut him off. "If you weren't such a sorry, spineless mess, if you had just a grain of sense, you'd have never gotten yourself into debt in the first place. The money is secondary. Right now I need to know what you did with the small, clay, baton-shaped thing you took out of my sock drawer. It had turning dials and looked pretty antique. What did you do with it?"

"I—I don't remember," Cory stammered.

Lily saw Sebastian's hand in his pocket turn into a fist, as if clutching something. "Is that so? Well maybe this will jog your memory." He pressed down on Cory's throat, cutting off the man's air for a moment. Cory's eyes bulged in panic and his hands scrabbled at Sebastian's hold. Before he could get too desperate, Sebastian let up again.

"Okay, okay!" Cory croaked, coughing and wheezing. "I think—I think maybe I do remember. I sold it to the antique shop in town. Didn't have a chance to unload it in Atlanta before I ra—I mean, before I came here."

Sebastian's grip on whatever was in his pocket loosened and his grim face broke into a smile as he stood up and let go of Cory.

"See, that wasn't too hard, was it, ol' buddy?"

Cory sat up, rubbing his throat and holding his head. He glared at Sebastian, somewhat braver now that he wasn't pinned down.

"You could've just asked nicely, jeeze. My head is killing me. I don't get why everyone's so excited about that piece of junk, like it was special or something."

Lily's ears perked at that, troubled by the implication. She stepped forward from her place in the doorway. "What do you mean 'everyone'? Has someone else been asking about it?"

Cory turned, focusing on her for the first time now that his life wasn't being threatened. He eyed her up and down and gave her what he probably thought was a charming smile, or as charming as one could get when hung over and nervous.

"Well, hey there, good lookin'—"

Sebastian's sound cuff to the head cut him off, almost knocking him over sideways onto the bed. Lily blushed, embarrassed.

"Keep a civil tongue in your head and answer her," Sebastian said, scowling fiercely.

"Oh jeeze, my head," Cory moaned, leaning forward and massaging his temples.

Lily took pity and gave him a moment to recover from the blow.

"Well?" she asked again, glancing sideways at Sebastian, who was fidgeting impatiently.

"Yeah, yeah. You guys are the second to show up asking about that weird clay thing. The first guy was just here a while ago. *He* didn't beat me up. Offered me money for it, then disappeared without a word when I said I'd sold it to the antique place." Cory sounded as disappointed as he looked at missing a chance to make easy money.

Lily exchanged a worried glance with Sebastian. Who else would know about the device, much less know where to look for it? Unless maybe it was Freddie?

"What did he look like?" Lily asked, noticing Sebastian glancing at his watch again.

"Oh, sh—" Sebastian started.

They vanished.

Lily blinked, confused. She stared at the empty room that, moments before, had contained two other people. And that wasn't even the most confusing thing about the scene before her. Everything had gone black and white and blurred around the edges, like an antique camera picture just a touch out of focus. She stepped back, stumbled, and caught herself against the wall of the room as her disoriented mind tried to adjust. She didn't sink through it as she leaned there, so the wall *was* solid. But she couldn't feel it. She couldn't feel anything at all for that matter. Or hear or smell. It was as if her senses had gone dead.

Still stumbling as her sense of balance attempted to readjust to the fuzzy, silent, not-there world around her, she made her way out of Cory's house. She tripped on the last porch step and fell to the gravel-strewn ground, hands and knees striking hard. It didn't hurt.

Rising was difficult. Gravity still worked, or at least she supposed it did since she wasn't floating. But the feeling of heaviness, that sense of being pulled toward the earth, was gone. It was the most disorienting and indescribable situation she'd ever experienced.

When she finally stood back on her feet, she looked up at the sky and fear struck her heart. The sky was gone. In its place was a transparent ceiling, like glass. Beyond it swirls of gray and white moved, pressing against the glass in ever-changing patterns as if some current drove them to and fro. These strange gyrations continued all the way to the horizon, making it look like she was inside a glass dome and all the world outside was swallowed up in a sea of swirling nothingness.

Where was she? What had happened to everyone else? If it had to do with the time loop, then why had Sebastian disappeared while she was left behind?

Feeling lost and on the edge of panic, she sat down, determined to get a grip. There was a logical, or at least magical, explanation for all this; she just needed to think. How she wished for her eduba and its depth of knowledge. But it wasn't there, so she'd have to do without.

Sitting cross-legged, hands resting on her thighs in her favorite meditative position, she closed her eyes to the swirling gray above and considered the problem.

One: there was a magical device looping time. Two: it seemed to be spatially bound, only covering the area of Pitts. Three: the magic of the loop didn't affect her when it reset, even though she was within range.

Wait a minute. She opened her eyes, looking down at her hands. Of course. She wore a personal ward, a series of dimmu-engraved beads woven into a bracelet that graced her wrist. It acted as a passive shield against targeted magic. That meant the lugal-nam's magic must be layered, probably a combination of an area affect spell that created and maintained the loop's boundary, and a targeted spell that reset the loop's timeline. Earlier, by some fluke, she'd entered an in-progress loop. But when the loop was reset, the spell that sent everyone back to the beginning had been blocked by her personal ward, unable to affect her.

So where was she now?

Lily looked around, trying to spot some detail that would give her a clue. Nothing in the Basement's library or her eduba had ever mentioned a place like this. Out of the corner of her eye, she caught a flicker of movement. A bird had just appeared out of the gray swirls, flying straight through what had appeared to be a solid glass ceiling. She followed the bird's flight, watching intently as it neared the other side of the dome. The bird did not pause or slow. It flew straight on, passing through the barrier and back into the gray swirls as if it didn't even see them. Well, perhaps it didn't. Perhaps, what appeared to her as glass was in fact a magical barrier, the time-loop's physical boundary that encircled Pitts. She could see it, and not beyond it, because she was still tied to the loop somehow. The bird paid it no mind because it didn't exist to the bird. The bird existed in real time, flying over an empty Pitts whose inhabitants were all caught up in the loop. Well, all except her. Physically, she was still here in Cory's yard about a half mile or so outside of town. But with respect to time, at least real time and the loop's time, she didn't exist. She had a *where*, but not a *when*, which was probably why her senses were going haywire. The gray world she saw around her was real time, flowing onward as normal. She could see it, but wasn't in it, and so couldn't influence or be influenced by it.

She shivered, trying not to dwell on the implications of being stuck in between realities. Though far from an expert on the theory of time manipulation, Lily remembered a few things. They all involved warnings against the danger of moving between time and getting lost. How would she ever get back?

She thought about taking off her ward but reconsidered halfway through reaching for it. There was no way to know what kind of raw power or magical anomalies were present in this in-between state. Taking off her ward might just as easily throw her into nothingness as get her home.

Sighing, she slumped forward and rested her head in her hands, propping her elbows on her knees. None of this made sense. How had she even gotten into this mess in the first place?

That thought made her sit up again. She considered it, doing some mental calculations.

The loop was supposed to be a closed system, yet both she and Sebastian had been pulled in. That wasn't supposed to happen. If tears or openings were showing up in the fabric of the magic, creating weak points, then the spell must be degrading. Depending on how many times the loop had been reset, and how old the device was, it made sense that the magic might be weakening. Like everything else in life, spells faded over time to varying degrees and either had to be renewed or sealed in an inactive state to retain their power. If the device's seal had been broken when it was activated, its power could be fading, drained by continual resets.

But who was using it? More important, did they realize the magic was fading? The implications of a time loop breaking apart while still in effect was chilling. People might be sucked out of the loop through weak points and left stranded in this in-between space. Worse, if the magic went haywire in the middle of a loop, it could throw everyone into nothingness. Three hundred and seven people, or whatever the actual population of Pitts was these days, could cease to exist.

Sebastian's words held a new meaning. Lives were indeed at stake.

Lily got up abruptly, wobbling somewhat as she struggled for balance. She was getting the hang of this gravity-yet-no-gravity thing, but it took concentration.

Now that she had an idea of what was going on, it was time to do something about it. She had to get back to town and check out that antique store. It was imperative to find the device as quickly as possible and stop whoever was using it from looping it again. If she could find a hint of its whereabouts, then all she had to do was re-enter the loop and track it down. She hoped against hope she could use her original entry point—the weak spot on Pitts's main street—to get back in and meet up with Sebastian.

She started off north, toward town, weaving back and forth unsteadily as she waded through the gray grass. Her passage left no mark, bent no blade, and left no imprint in the soil. It was as if she wasn't even there.

Lily had no idea how long it took her to get to town. Her cell phone, safely in her back jeans pocket, had frozen, probably because of all the magical interference. It might have been five minutes, or five hours. Or maybe time didn't exist in this in-between space.

When she finally got there, however, everything was exactly as it had been before. The cars were still parked along the main street, including hers, the "OPEN" sign still hung in the 5 and Dime, and the fan was still rotating back and forth in the antique store. The fact that everything now appeared black and white and fuzzy around the edges simply added to the eeriness of the scene.

She made her way to the antique store and pushed through the front door. The gray door didn't move at her touch, the same way the grass didn't move as she walked through the field. Neither did she pass insubstantially through the closed door. Yet, somehow, she found herself on the other side.

Looking around, she almost forgot her dire situation. The clutter of old furniture and lamps, bookshelves of embossed tomes, and cases full of trinkets made her heart flutter with excitement. She was in front of a corner bookcase, reaching toward a particularly magnificent-looking copy of *Great Expectations,* before she remembered that not only was she not there to read, but she probably couldn't take it off the bookshelf, anyway.

With a sigh, she turned toward the rear of the store, weaving in and out of piles of antiques to see if she could find where the owner kept his inventory records. As she rounded the last pile, she ran smack dab into a rather solid-yet-not-solid something and was thrown off balance. She had to devote all her concentration to staying upright. Once she had her balance back, she took a good look at what she'd run into and nearly fell over again in shock. Filling up the narrow space between the pile of things she'd rounded and the long glass case that served as a counter stood a man. Despite the force with which she'd made contact, he seemed oblivious to her presence. Like everything else in the store, he was gray and fuzzy around the edges, leading her to assume he existed in real time, outside the loop. That meant she couldn't touch or influence him.

To test her theory, she cautiously approached and waved a hand in front of his face as he leaned over the glass case, examining an open ledger. He didn't blink or seem to notice her hand at all. She tried touching him. There was something there that her hand couldn't push past, but she wasn't really touching him. The fabric of his sleeve—he wore a very expensive Italian suit, by the look of it—didn't dent in as she poked at it with her finger.

Taking a step back, Lily examined him curiously, watching as he turned a page and continued reading through the ledger. There was something almost familiar about him, yet she was sure she'd never seen him before. Or had she? Perhaps he simply looked like someone she'd known once, but couldn't remember. He certainly wasn't Freddie, not if

Sebastian's older brother looked anything like Sebastian himself. This man was solidly built and of medium height, not tall and lanky like her friend. He also had a Roman nose and decidedly patrician features in contrast to Sebastian's less angular, boyish face.

Besides his expensive-looking clothes and perfectly trimmed hair, beard, and goatee, the man seemed normal enough. Except the normal she was used to in Atlanta was distinctly out of place in a backwater like Pitts. Here, the fine clothes and immaculate grooming screamed money and class, both rare sights in this town. She looked closer and noticed a large ring on the forefinger of his left hand. It was set with a gigantic, pitch-black stone—onyx most likely—and the thick band was heavily engraved with dimmu runes.

Lily felt a jolt of excitement mixed with dread. This man could simply be a collector of fine antiques, but her gut told her he was a wizard. That ring looked like a power anchor, similar to the amulet attached to her ward bracelet, only much stronger, judging by those runes. If he was a wizard, he was probably here for the same reason she was: the artifact Sebastian had lost. Perhaps this was the "someone" who'd offered Cory money for the lugal-nam.

Trying not to touch him, even though he wouldn't know, Lily inched in close and peered over him at the ledger. Everything had been written in a spidery, neat hand. The ledger listed each item in the shop followed by its details such as the seller, cost, date of purchase, description, buyer, date of sale, and profit. The items were numbered, and papers scattered around the ledger were stapled with Polaroid photographs of antiques, each one meticulously labeled with the item number and date. Obviously, the man before her was searching through the ledger and pictures for the lugal-nam.

Taking a closer look at the page the man was currently examining, Lily realized he wasn't just searching for it. He'd found it. It was hard to see the picture, as it lay on the opposite side of the thick ledger from her, but the item in it was unmistakable: a cylinder-shaped tube about six inches long made up of rotating pieces like a combination lock. Just then the man leaned closer to the picture, blocking Lily's view as he squinted at it, so she switched her attention to the line in the ledger on which his finger rested. It listed the item's details, as well as a date and amount of sale. She peered closer, heartbeat quickening, trying to read sideways around the man's hand. It appeared the antique-store owner had sold the lugal-nam about two weeks ago in early June to a man named Rob. She couldn't see the last name, covered as it was by the man's finger.

Though doubtful it would help, she reached forward anyway, trying to shift the man's hand so she could see the writing underneath. As she reached, the amulet hanging from her wrist brushed against the stone on the man's ring, and for the first time since she'd been thrown into this in-between time, she *felt* something, like a jolt of power. Based on the startled jerk of the man's hand, he felt it, too. He looked at the offending limb, perplexed, then raised his head to peer around him. Lily knew he couldn't see her, but she still paused only long enough to read the last name the man's finger had covered, before shrinking back.

Turning her direction, the man's gaze passed over her, then swung back and lingered. Lily shivered. He wasn't looking *at* her exactly, but she felt sure he could see, or sense, her there. The puzzled wrinkle of his forehead deepened to a frown, and she saw his lips move, though she couldn't hear his words. Not waiting around to find out if he was merely talking to himself or casting a spell, Lily fled the antique store. She had what she needed. Now if only she could get back in the time loop where it would do her some good.

Chapter 3

Here We Go Again

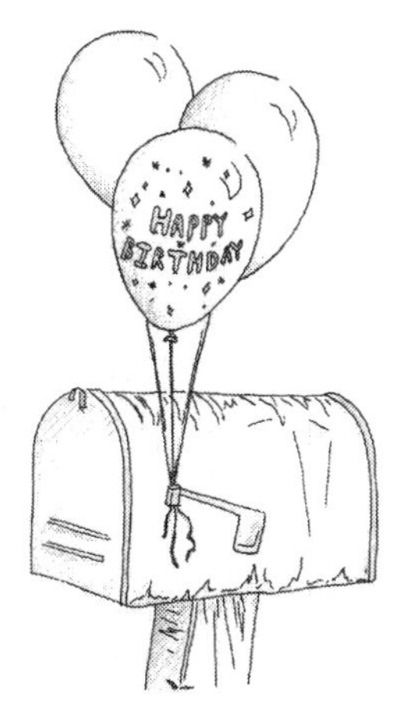

OUT ON THE STREET ONCE MORE, LILY RETRACED HER STEPS TO THE curb where she'd first entered the loop. A quick glance at the antique store assured her the strange man hadn't followed her out.

Relieved, she closed her eyes and tried to remember how she'd entered the loop the first time. There'd been a sensation of being pulled sideways and squeezed, as if she'd been forced through a narrow crack between realities. Such a crack shouldn't exist. Its presence weakened the integrity of the time loop. But if it got her back where she needed to go, she'd worry about the rest later.

Taking a deep, calming breath, Lily relaxed and sank into a meditative state, opening herself to the Source to feel the currents of magic around her. If she focused hard enough, maybe she could find...

There.

In that gray world of muted senses, she felt the barest hint of something. It was a slight shift in the aether before her, like feeling a draft in a cave. She held tight to it, seeing the trickle of magic in her mind as it seeped through the crack before her.

Lily stepped toward it and...

Stumbled.

Scowling, she turned and stared at the spot where the crack should've been. The asphalt was unsurprisingly immune to her glare, so she sighed and stepped back up onto the curb to try again. And again.

At one point during her attempts, the man from the antique store emerged onto the sidewalk, disrupting her concentration. She watched nervously as he surveyed the seemingly empty street. Though his gaze swept in her direction, it didn't linger. After a few moments he set off east, toward the outskirts of town. Knowing they were after the same thing, Lily redoubled her efforts, anxious to find the lugal-nam before it fell into the wrong hands.

After several more fruitless attempts, she stopped herself. She was missing something. Recalling the memory of her first passage, she scrutinized every detail. Then it dawned on her: the pull through had been *sideways*. Her physical movements were irrelevant since it was the loop's magic which had pulled her sideways from one timeline to another.

Armed with this newfound discovery, she readied herself again. The draft of magic tickled her senses as she focused on it and carefully, without moving, stepped sideways through time and...

Emerged onto a sunlit street curb.

A wave of sensation bombarded her, driving her to the ground where she sat, momentarily dazed. Cars trundled by on the street and a few passersby looked at her strangely. She ignored them all. Closing her eyes, she reveled in the feeling of rough cement beneath her hands, the smell of the hot summer air, and the warmth of sunshine on her skin.

"Lily!"

A familiar cry came from across the street, and Lily's eyes snapped open. She was intensely relieved to see Sebastian running toward her—an unfamiliar feeling, since his appearance usually evoked annoyance and exasperation.

Wobbling unsteadily, she rose in time to be swept up in a tight hug, throwing her completely off balance once more. The hug was brief, giving her shocked brain no chance to protest before Sebastian relaxed his embrace to hold her at arm's length, his expression relieved.

"Good grief, Lil, you scared me to death! What happened?" Sebastian's words came out in a breathless rush. "You weren't there when the time loop restarted. I've spent hours looking for you! I was worried you might have gotten stuck or lost somewhere. I didn't know what to do."

"Calm down, for heaven's sake," Lily said, trying to regain a semblance of composure despite Sebastian's death grip on her shoulders. "I'm perfectly fine. I *was* stuck, but I found my way back. If you'll stop squeezing me to death, I'll explain."

"Oh, sorry," he said, dropping his hands self-consciously.

There was a moment of awkward silence.

"So, um, shall we sit?" Lily asked, gesturing to a bench further down the sidewalk.

"Yeah!" Sebastian agreed, seeming relieved.

Sitting down, Lily explained all about the space in-between, the strange man, and how she'd managed to return.

She also noted, with no little amount of annoyance, that Sebastian's pant legs were now clean and free of the mud and stickers they'd tramped through following Grimmold, as if it had never happened. Her pants and shoes were still covered with it. While she spoke, she worked on brushing off the dried flakes of muck.

When she finished, Sebastian's expression was troubled.

"So, you think the guy in the antique shop was a wizard?" he asked.

Lily shrugged. "There's no way to be sure, but I doubt anyone could've acquired a power anchor like that ring otherwise, especially one so powerful. It's not as if you can buy one at the local 'wizard-mart.' You have to construct it yourself. It's a deeply personalized item, and it never functions as well for another wizard. The only exception is a blood descendant. They've been known to be passed down within wizard families. Regardless, he must be a wizard to have entered the loop to find Cory, then exited again to search the antique store. I have no notion how he's doing it. Then again, I have never studied time magic. It's a dangerous field. Most people die fiddling with time or disappear, never to be seen again."

Lily fell silent, her thoughts troubled. *She* was meddling with time, and historical precedent did not predict a favorable outcome. All the more reason to find the artifact and escape this loop as soon as possible.

"Well," she began again, "now that we're caught up, it's time we—"

"Oh no! What time is it?" Sebastian cried, looking at his watch and jumping up from the bench in almost the same moment.

"Wha—"

"Be right back!" Sebastian dashed up the street, leaving Lily with her mouth agape in astonished question. He seemed to be headed for a young girl coming toward them across the street. Her braided hair, adorned with bright beads, bounced as she walked, and she licked happily on an ice cream cone probably acquired moments before at the 5 and Dime store behind her. The dripping treat left white drops of melted confection on her hand and wrist that contrasted sharply with the girl's ebony skin.

Lily couldn't imagine what Sebastian was up to. Though a car was driving down the street toward them, it was far enough away to not pose a threat to the girl. Yet, Sebastian didn't slow.

As she watched, he scooped the girl up in his arms and out of the approaching car's path just as it materialized exactly where she'd been seconds before. It was as if the car had teleported forward. The startled driver screeched to a halt, and Lily noticed the car now sat barely a dozen feet from the lamppost marking the crack she'd originally come through.

Setting the girl gently down, Sebastian spoke to the driver who, window lowered, was most likely apologizing for not seeing them in the road. As the car drove off, Lily watched him escort the girl back across the street. Before leaving, he dug in his pocket and handed her some change, an obvious apology for the ice cream cone now lying smushed in the middle of the road.

"What in the world was that about?" Lily asked as he returned to the bench.

"What did it look like?" Sebastian grinned, obviously pleased with himself.

"Well, it looked like a time warp. The crack we both came through is skewing the normal flow, creating pockets of distortion. It's like I told you: the magic holding this loop together is weakening."

"Well, yeah, that too," Sebastian agreed. "But did you notice my handy little save? I saw her get hit a few loops ago. Couldn't let it happen again, now could I?"

Lily sighed, exasperated. "Yes, I saw it. You did a tremendous job. I'm pleased she's safe. But don't you see what's happening? Saving one girl won't be enough if we can't find this device before everything spins out of control."

That made him pause. "Ah. Yes. I see the problem there... so what are we going to do?"

"We need to locate Rob Smith. He's the one who bought the device from the antique store."

"Good thing you got his name. The old grouch who owns the place wouldn't tell me a thing. Tight-lipped as a clam."

Lily cocked an eyebrow. "Clams don't have lips."

"I know that, but they...oh, never mind. So how are we going to find out where this guy lives? The people in this town seem pretty shy of outsiders."

"Is that so?" Lily asked, affecting a shocked expression which failed to disguise her smirk. "Has the unthinkable happened and your charm failed you? How rude of it."

"Oh, shut up. I'd like to see you do any better."

"I don't have to. It's called a phone book, genius. You have heard of those, haven't you?"

"Er, yes. There's that," Sebastian admitted, sheepish.

Lily rolled her eyes. With everything going digital these days, people often forgot written records did, in fact, still exist. She didn't care how convenient digital content was, nothing could ever replace the feel and smell of a book in hand. Fortunately, most old-fashioned people agreed with her. As small and quaint as this town was, there were sure to be plenty of phone books about.

"One of the shops around here should have one. Come on." Lily said.

Sebastian bowed theatrically, extending his hand toward the shops across the street, inviting her to take the lead. "As you're the queen of a papery domain, I'll leave the finding of any and all books in your capable hands."

With a snort of amusement, Lily started across the street, Sebastian trailing behind.

Their phone book search had proved fruitful. They now stood on a little neighborhood street looking at Rob Smith's house, a mere four blocks away from Pitts's main thoroughfare. In any larger town, Lily would have despaired at finding the owner of such a common name. But he was one of only two Rob Smiths listed. The other lived so far out in the country they decided it would be outside the geographical reach of the time loop.

Rob's house was small but tidy. A somewhat dented white sedan was parked in the driveway beside a mailbox adorned with a handful of "Happy Birthday" balloons. Several other vehicles were parked on the street to either side of the driveway. Sounds of children's laughter drifted on the summer air, coming from the fenced-in yard behind the house.

"Looks like we're about to crash someone's birthday party," Sebastian observed.

"Mmm," Lily agreed absentmindedly. She was busy looking inward, feeling for something, anything, that would indicate this particular house was the source of the loop's magic.

"Well, I guess this is it," Sebastian said, not bothered by her silence. "Let's go see if our 'time-lord' is to be found amidst the balloons and streamers. Leave the talking to me, Lil. I've been known to charm snakes with my voice alone. This should be a piece of cake. We might even get some actual cake out of the deal, if all goes well." He winked at her before striding forward up the tidy walkway to the front porch.

Rolling her eyes, Lily followed, forbearing to mention his lack of success with the antique dealer.

The man who answered Sebastian's ring at the door was middle-aged, with short-cropped hair and a face lined with care. His welcoming expression turned to a look of guarded curiosity upon seeing two strangers at his door. No doubt he'd expected to greet another birthday party guest.

"Mr. Rob Smith?" Sebastian asked politely, a tentative air obvious in his tone.

"Yeah. What do y'all want?" the man asked.

Sebastian nodded in greeting. "Good afternoon, sir. We're very sorry to interrupt your celebration, and we don't wish to intrude, but might we have a moment of your time?"

"What for?" Rob asked, eyes narrowing in suspicion.

"Well," Sebastian said, hesitating as he carefully evaluated his word choice. "We have a bit of a problem and were hoping you could help us. In fact, you're the only one who *can* help us." Lily noticed that one of his hands was curled around something in his pocket, just like when he'd interrogated Cory.

Sebastian paused, giving Rob a chance to comment, but the man remained stony and silent.

"You see," Sebastian continued, "We're looking for something you recently bought at the antique store in town, a sort of cylinder made out of clay with rotating dials. It's a family heirloom of great sentimental value that was mistakenly sold. It would mean a great deal to my family to get it back. Have you seen it?"

Rob's expression changed from guarded to angry. "I already told the other guy I don't know what you're talking about. Y'all had better stop harrassin' me or I'll call the sheriff. It's my son's birthday, for God's sake. Now get off my porch!"

With that, he slammed the door in their faces, and they heard the sound of a turning lock. A moment of stunned silence followed in which Lily and Sebastian shared a worried look.

"The other guy?" Lily asked.

"I think your wizard friend has beaten us to the punch again. Though with no better luck, it seems." Sebastian turned and left the porch, going to peer through one of the front windows.

"Stop that!" Lily hissed, grasping his arm and pulling him back onto the porch. "Do you want him to see you and call the cops right now? That wouldn't help our situation. We need to persuade him to talk to us. If we wait for the next loop, he won't remember speaking to us, right? We can try a different tack."

"Maybe," Sebastian mused. "But why wait? Can't you just wiggle your fingers, do a bit of magic, and get us in? Or say a special word and summon the device, like the boy with the glasses and funny scar on his forehead in that kids' book?"

Lily gave him a withering look. "No, in fact, I can't. This is why we wizards prefer to keep to ourselves, because everybody reads made-up stories about magic and assumes it's as easy as waving a wand and saying a few words. They'd ask us to do all sorts of ridiculous things."

"Well, isn't it that easy?" Sebastian asked, giving her a knowing grin.

"I mean, yes. In a way. But not like you're implying. We do use words of power to shape the magic, and there are many well-studied spells which, if done right, give predictable results. But unlike in stories, magic is *part* of nature, it doesn't defy it. The only reason mundanes call what wizards do "magic" is because it's science they don't understand yet. It took centuries of experimentation to perfect the spells we know about, and creating new ones can be dangerous."

"If you say so," Sebastian replied, shrugging his shoulders as they left the porch and headed back to the road.

"The question is moot anyway," she said. "I don't think I can use magic within the loop."

"Really?" he asked, brow furrowing.

With a sigh, Lily shook her head. "Ever since I entered the loop, my connection to the Source hasn't felt right, much less stable. I don't know what effect the loop may have on my spells. They might work, or they might spin wildly out of control. I'd rather not try unless the situation is desperate. We should have plenty of time to explore other less risky options. On the bright side, if I can't use magic, hopefully the other wizard can't, either."

Sebastian clapped his hands and rubbed them together. "Okay. Back to plan B, I guess. We'll see what we can do in the next loop."

They whittled away the hours until the loop reset, Sebastian's relaxed unconcern contrasting with Lily's barely suppressed worry. At the reset, her transition to the gray in-between world was much less disorienting now that she knew what to expect. Before seeking out the crack through which she would join Sebastian, she took some time to explore Rob Smith's house. As she'd suspected, she found nothing of interest or value, only a gray, blurry version of the house in real time, devoid of inhabitants or evidence of the device that started it all.

Not only did she not find anything at the house, but on the way back to Pitts she kept seeing disconcerting flickering out of the corner of her eye. It was as if the barrier between timelines was weakening in places beyond her perception. The anomaly worried her.

Her second time through the crack took fewer tries, and she was soon back on the sunny main street of Pitts. This time she found Sebastian waiting for her on the bench just down the street. Obviously bored of waiting, he was playing with his coin, though he put it away as soon as he saw her.

"Finally," he said once she was in earshot. "What took you so long?"

"I searched Mr. Smith's house, but there was nothing useful." Lily shrugged.

"Pity. So what's our angle on Rob this time?"

"I think we shouldn't be so direct, and you should let me do the talking." Lily peered over her glasses at Sebastian, adopting the look of a teacher studying her student. "Obviously, your handsome charm doesn't do the trick."

"And your bookish awkwardness will?" he replied in a teasing tone.

Lily lifted her chin in a show of confidence she didn't quite feel. Confrontation wasn't her strong point, but she had to try.

"I'll approach him as a professional and make my affiliation with Agnes Scott College known up front. That should make him less suspicious."

Sebastian shrugged. "It's as good a plan as any." Standing, he stretched, then motioned in the direction of Rob's house. "Might as well get it over with."

"What about the little girl?" Lily asked as she stood up, recalling the last time-loop's events.

"Her? I gallantly snatched her from danger a good thirty minutes ago. You took longer to show up, remember?"

"Oh," she said.

Sebastian grinned, giving her a slap on the back. "Well, let's go crash a birthday party…again."

This time Lily rang the doorbell, having instructed Sebastian to wait on the steps. As it opened, however, before she even had a chance to speak, Rob started yelling.

"What the heck do y'all think you're doing? I told you to leave me alone! I swear, if I find y'all or that other guy on my doorstep one more time I'll call the sheriff. Now beat it!"

Completely taken aback, Lily barely got out a "well, excuse me" before the man abruptly slammed the door in their faces. Again.

The moment of stunned silence was even deeper this time as Lily worked to regain her composure and Sebastian made only a small effort to hide his smirk.

"Oh, hush!" she exclaimed, having wheeled around and spotted his ill-disguised smile. She stomped forward, dragging him after her as they retreated once more to the road. "Don't you see? This has nothing to do with anything I said. He remembered us from the last loop, and he's the only one in this whole mess besides you and me who does. That means he *must* be the one resetting the loop, because only the one who initiates the magic would keep their memories."

"How do you know?" Sebastian asked.

"Time magic wouldn't make any sense otherwise, now would it? The person controlling the magic needs to be fully aware, or else they can't manage the spell. There would be provisions written into any such spell to ensure the caster kept their memories. I don't know how he's doing it, though, unless Rob is a wizard himself. Such a device would have to be initially activated by a live connection to the Source, though I suppose the creators could have written controlling runes to allow secondary manual control once the initial spell was activated."

"Okay," Sebastian said, rolling his eyes, "now that everything is clear as mud, could you repeat that in English?"

Lily sighed. "The magic of the loop wouldn't reset the memories of the person who was using the device. A wizard would have to be the one resetting it, since it needs magic to work, unless the device was built to be controlled by a physical switch once it was active. Like pushing buttons on a remote."

"Ah, that's what you meant. So, do you think Rob is a wizard?"

Lily shook her head. "No. Wizards can't hide from each other. It's hard to describe, but being connected to the Source makes you sensitive to others who use it. There are masking spells, but they have tells, too. The only reason I wasn't sure if the man in the antique store was a wizard is because I wasn't in the same time dimension as he was. I couldn't feel anything, much less his connection to the Source.

"What if *he* activated it?" Sebastian mused.

"And then let it slip through his fingers? Not likely. If that wizard gets his hands on it, he'll make sure it stays there. No, there's a part of this we're missing."

Sebastian frowned. "So how are we going to get this guy to listen to us if he remembers everything? Why not just break in and take the device?"

She looked askance at him. "And risk him attacking us in self-defense? That's begging for trouble. I think we simply need to be more insistent and explain the danger. I'm sure he'll be reasonable if he understands what's at stake. He could be looping it by accident."

"Hmm. I wouldn't count on it," Sebastian said doubtfully.

"Well, we have to try," insisted Lily.

"Be my guest, Ms. Professional. A woman is less threatening anyway, so maybe he won't call the cops on you. I'll stay here."

Lily gave him a look of consternation but couldn't deny his logic. "Fine, if you insist. Somebody has to fix this mess, after all. Heaven forbid it be you."

Without waiting to see his reaction, she turned and marched back up the drive. This whole situation thoroughly irritated her and she was quite ready to pound sense into *somebody*, she didn't care who.

She rang the doorbell over and over, not stopping until she saw the doorknob turn. Expecting him to come out shouting, she began talking at once to cut off his anticipated tirade.

"Mr. Smith, please. My name is Lily Singer and I'm the archives manager at Agnes Scott College in Atlanta. I am aware you're using some sort of device to loop time, and I have to warn you everyone here is in serious danger. We need to talk about this."

Standing in the now open doorway, Rob regarded her with a stubborn expression. "You're out of your mind, lady. I got no clue what you're talking about."

"Yes you do," Lily insisted, "You can't pretend you're unaware. This time looping has to stop. The magic holding everything together is weakening and you're putting everyone's life at risk if it fails."

Except for a brief flash of uncertainty, Rob's expression remained set. Most people scoffed or protested at the mention of magic. He did neither, making Lily even more certain he was responsible for the loop.

"I got no idea what you're talking about," he repeated, though the look of knowing in his eyes belied his statement. "We're celebrating my boy's birthday, and we'll *keep* celebrating it for as long as we want. Ain't no harm in that. Beats me where you get your crazy ideas, but take 'em somewhere else. I'm calling the sheriff."

Lily suffered the door being slammed in her face a third time. Letting out a sigh of frustration, she turned to rejoin Sebastian.

"That went well," he observed, making an effort to keep his face straight this time.

"That idiot!" Lily fumed. "He knows, *he knows* what he's doing and he doesn't care. He's using a dangerous and unstable magical artifact he knows nothing about and ignoring any possibility of danger. What a complete and utter…utter…" she spluttered to a stop, at a loss for words to express the depth of her disgust.

Sebastian gently took her shoulders and steered her down the street, away from the house. "Maybe he has a good reason."

"What possible reason could there be to endanger the whole town so your child can have a perpetual birthday party? His son won't even remember!"

"No idea," Sebastian said, shrugging, "but I suggest we make ourselves scarce. If he really did call the cops, waiting for the next loop won't wipe his memory but it sure will wipe theirs."

They spent the remainder of that loop talking about strategies for getting the lugal-nam, as well as how to end the loop once they got it. Ideally, they could wait for the loop to run out and then rejoin real time. But in case the spell wouldn't dissipate on its own, Lily assured him they could break the device to end the spell. She knew from experience as soon as dimmu runes were broken, they lost the magic cast on them.

They also kept an eye on the street leading to Rob's house, in case the other wizard showed up. Once the loop reset, Lily even spent time searching the in-between space for him, though she was hindered by the constant flickering. It had become worse and was now accompanied by a strange shifting of time and space. Again and again, she took a step and was suddenly a few yards away from where she'd been seconds before. Once she was transported a whole block, ending up in the middle of the street. With how unstable the time loop was becoming, she was surprised the little girl Sebastian had saved was the only one hurt so far. The continuity of the in-between space especially was crumbling, and soon it might no longer be passable. They were running out of time. How many more loops could they survive before everything broke apart?

Spurred on by this new sense of urgency, she gave up her fruitless search and rejoined Sebastian inside the loop just in time to watch him save the little girl again. She even managed a smile when the girl's ice cream splattered itself all over Sebastian instead of the pavement. It wasn't anything a few wet napkins couldn't fix, but his affronted look, as if he'd been personally insulted by the ice cream, was priceless.

When they approached Rob's house for a third time, Lily's heart sank. A sheriff's cruiser sat in Rob's driveway, and the sheriff himself stood on the front porch talking with Rob. An older man, the officer had the look of a bodybuilder gone to seed. His impressive girth spoke more of desk-riding and paper-filing than fieldwork.

Lily pulled Sebastian off the road and behind some bushes, shielding them from view.

"Now what?" she asked, exasperated and utterly sick of the whole affair. "We can't keep waiting for another loop. I don't know how much longer the magic will hold."

Sebastian looked thoughtful. "What we need," he finally said, "is a distraction. Something to keep the sheriff busy while you talk some sense into that thickhead."

Lily looked around, at a loss. "What, though? What would be disturbing enough to get the sheriff's attention, yet not endanger innocent bystanders?"

A glint of mischief entered Sebastian's eyes, and he grinned widely. "You leave that to me."

"Wait, what are you going to do?" she asked, suspicious.

"Never you mind. I'll take care of it."

"But what if Mr. Smith calls more cops?" Lily protested.

Sebastian shook his head. "In a town this small, I bet there isn't even a proper police station. It'll just be the sheriff's office and he's probably the only one staffing it. Besides, we're in a closed loop, remember? He can't exactly call for backup."

Lily looked doubtful, but she didn't have a better idea so she nodded in agreement. "I guess we don't have a choice."

"Don't you worry your pretty little head, Lil. Stay out of sight until the sheriff is gone and then talk some sense into that idiot. If it doesn't work, I'll meet you in the usual place.

If it does, well, I guess we'll both have to see what happens next."

Annoyed at his continued misuse of her name, Lily pursed her lips but didn't protest, knowing now was not the time.

"Okay," she replied. "But what do you mean by 'meet you'? Where are you going?"

Instead of answering, Sebastian simply winked before sauntering off down the street toward Rob's house.

Throwing up her hands in resignation, Lily started off after him. She dodged from house to house and bush to bush to keep out of sight until she was across the street and one house down from Rob's.

She watched apprehensively as Sebastian approached the pair in that casual yet confident way of his, moving as if he owned the very ground he walked upon. She'd seen him use this move to get into all sorts of places and wished she had such casual grace.

As he engaged the two men in conversation, Lily strained to hear their words but could only make out Rob's angry and the sheriff's placating tones. Sebastian spoke again and his words made the sheriff stiffen. The officer's demeanor changed from laid-back to official and he spoke harshly.

Whatever the sheriff said must have seemed funny to Sebastian, because he threw back his head and laughed with gusto. Predictably, it was not well received by either Rob or the sheriff. Rob's frown deepened and he started yelling, while the sheriff's face turned beet red. The officer gestured angrily and, by his body language, was obviously demanding Sebastian get lost and never show his face in Pitts again. But Sebastian kept talking, his tone mocking and brimming with insult. To Lily's astonishment, he even stepped closer and poked the man's ample stomach, probably making some joke about cops and donuts.

That, apparently, was the last straw. With a fierce scowl and barking command, the sheriff grabbed the offending limb prodding his person. Using his advantage in weight and bulk along with some impressive joint manipulation, he spun Sebastian around and cuffed him, speaking authoritatively. The sheriff then frog-marched her friend down the porch steps and to the cruiser, unceremoniously loading him into the partitioned back seat and slamming the door. He spoke a few words to Rob still up on the porch, then heaved himself into the cab and drove off toward town.

The silence following the vehicle's departure was broken only by the sound of a door shutting as Rob went back into his house.

For a while, Lily just stood there, thinking. Sebastian had said he would distract the sheriff, not get himself arrested. Now she had to worry about finding the lugal-nam *and* getting her friend out of jail. Great, just great.

With a sigh, she steeled herself and headed toward Rob's house. She was no good at this game, and she knew it. Her domain was the quiet, orderly walls of a library, not parties and strangers' porches. Have a stack of periodicals to file or a complicated spell to research? She was your woman. But arguing and conflict management were not her cup of tea. Besides her politely professional co-workers and an occasional misbehaving student, she rarely had contact with other adults, preferring to keep her own company, surrounded by books. She talked more to her cat, Sir Kipling, than she did to any human, except perhaps Sebastian, who didn't seem to mind her awkward, sarcastic, and sometimes cold behavior.

But reality didn't care that she hated confrontation with strangers. With Sebastian keeping the sheriff busy, it was up to her to save the day. Her situation was complicated by her reluctance to use magic, lest it backfire. She'd only been spell-casting for seven years, yet in that time it had become an integral part of her, and she felt naked without it.

To bolster her confidence, she adopted her "death stare," reserved for anyone caught mistreating her library books. Despite her relative youth, she was regarded with a healthy respect and not a little bit of fear by the student body. Her strict rules, fierce scowls, and uncanny ability to know when students were misbehaving—thanks to some well-placed detection spells—had earned her nicknames such as "Book Nazi," "Madam Killjoy," and "Ye Old Bat." She suspected the last two were holdovers from when her predecessor, Madam Barrington, had been archives manager.

Well, if she could cow a library full of unruly students, she could manage one stubborn man. It couldn't be that hard, could it?

Chapter 4

Nothing Lasts Forever

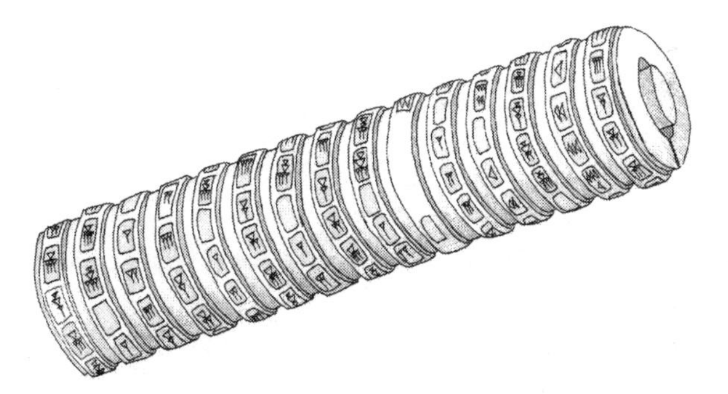

"LILY. LILY! CAN YOU HEAR ME? WAKE UP!"

For the life of her, Lily couldn't figure out why someone was yelling. She was just lying here, having a nice nap…

Lily sat bolt upright.

"What? Where am I? What's going on?"

The small crowd of people around her backed up, expressions ranging from relieved to disturbed.

"Alright, show's over, guys. She's fine. Must have been heat stroke or something," Sebastian said, waving dismissively at the crowd. Crouching by her elbow, he continued in a whisper. "Stand up and walk with me, but act weak like you just fainted."

Leaning heavily on Sebastian's strong arm—her weakness was no act—they made their way to a familiar bench down the street. Disoriented memories of what had happened were trickling back, and she didn't like them one bit. Something was missing, but she couldn't think what.

Sebastian made a show of helping her sit down and get comfortable. Then he produced a bottle of water.

"Drink, or you really will faint from heat stroke."

Squinting up at the hot noonday sun, she accepted the bottle and drank.

"So…what *did* happen?" Sebastian asked as he sat down next to her.

Lily massaged her temple with her free hand, trying to think back. "What day is it?" she asked, then shook her head at her own silly question. "I mean, what day is it in relation to you getting arrested?"

"It's the next loop. I came as soon as I could and found you lying on the sidewalk surrounded by a crowd of people. I don't think you'd been there long."

Sighing, Lily leaned back against the bench and held the still-cool bottle of water to her forehead, trying to remember.

That's when she noticed her bare wrist. "Oh no!" she exclaimed, sitting up suddenly and looking around in distress.

"What?" Sebastian asked, startled.

"My ward bracelet, it's gone!" Though the bracelet itself had been a gift from her mentor, the amulet on it was a family heirloom from her mother—the one thing her mother had forced her to take when she'd left home after their argument. She'd made Lily promise to always wear it. Not until Madam Barrington took her under her wing and opened her eyes to magic did she discover what it actually was. Lily supposed her mother had recognized she couldn't keep Lily from her heritage forever and had wanted her to be prepared with the tools she needed.

Jumping up, or at least trying to and wobbling a bit on the way to vertical, Lily hurried back up the street to the lamppost, Sebastian close behind. After a bit of searching, she found her bracelet nestled next to the concrete curb. Picking it up, they both stared at it. The braided rope of the bracelet was still intact, and her power-anchor amulet looked only slightly scratched. But the metal clasp and ward beads were all cracked and blackened.

Lily's shoulders slumped as the memories filtered back. "Mr. Smith wouldn't talk to me or let me in, so I tried to do a spell. I knew it was dangerous, but nothing else was working. If the loop had been stable, it might have been fine. But with everything shifting around so much I lost control of my link to the Source. The backlash broke my ward and that must have sent me back here, to the time and place I last entered the loop."

"Well, at least you're still here," Sebastian said, steering her back toward the bench. "You said before you were afraid if you took off the ward, you might disappear into nowhere. Plus, the ward did its job and protected you from the backlash. That's something, right?"

She nodded but still caressed the blackened beads sadly as she leaned back against the bench. Madam Barrington's gift had been precious as well as powerful. But at least this gave her a reason to make her own. She would just have to be very cautious until then.

"Hey, chin up," Sebastian said. "If you're not careful, Officer Lardgut may arrest you for public gloominess."

Looking up at his attempted joke, she saw a smile spread across his face.

"What are you grinning about?" she asked, perturbed. She'd failed to get the lugal-nam, been knocked unconscious by magic backlash, and lost her ward. Now here he was, grinning like a baboon.

"Oh nothing, nothing," he said. "It's just, you're safe, so crisis past. And I've been wanting to do that for *years*."

"Do what for years?"

Sebastian laughed. "Mouth off to a cop! Man, that was fun. I've had so many cop jokes bouncing around in my head for ages, that sheriff never stood a chance."

Remembering his misadventure of the previous loop, Lily rolled her eyes, not joining in his laughter.

"Aw, come on." Sebastian gave her a playful shove. "I'm grateful for all that 'to protect and serve,' but they can be a pain sometimes, roughing you up and being a bully just because they can. Haven't you ever wanted to mouth off to a cop? Not even a little?"

"I, unlike some people, have never found myself in a position to need to," Lily said, expression arch. No need to mention her one disastrous attempt at partying during college, the first and last time she'd ever gotten drunk. Then it had been more about wanting to kiss the cop than mouth off to him. She'd avoided alcohol ever since.

Sebastian laughed again, amused by the implied insult. "You could use a good mouthing off, Lily. It might loosen you up a bit."

"Humph," she snorted. "I have no desire to be loose. Politeness and decorum are traits sadly lacking in our current time. I'll have no part in any rabble-rousing."

"Rabble-rousing, huh? So what do you call exploding magic and breaking into people's houses? Tea-time frolics?"

Lily gave him a withering look but ignored the question. "What took you so long to get here, anyway?" she asked, still annoyed.

"The first time I entered the loop it was already mid- to late morning, so every time it resets, that's when I go back to."

"Well, we don't have the luxury of try, fail, repeat anymore. It's time we—"

"Oh no! What time is it?" Sebastian cried, looking at his watch and jumping up from the bench in almost the same moment.

"Wha—"

"Be right back!"

Lily watched him rush off, noticing for the first time that neither of them remembered the little girl in time to stop her from crossing the street in the first place. Sebastian always remembered just in time to save her from the car, and he always said the same thing. Maybe they were more influenced by the repetition of time than they thought, even though they were aware of it.

Then, out of nowhere, the memory of children playing in Rob's backyard flashed before her eyes and she sat up straight, thoughts whirling. The last piece of the puzzle suddenly slid into place and Lily realized they'd been going about this wrong from the start, trying to force their way in when what they needed was someone on the inside…

"That's it!" she yelled, jumping up and running to join Sebastian by the lamppost as he brushed off the little girl from their dive to safety.

Both her friend and the girl looked up in confusion.

Ignoring Sebastian, Lily crouched down to the girl's eye level. "Hi there. Are you okay? You're not hurt, are you?" she asked gently.

The little girl shook her head shyly. She looked to be eight or nine years old and had the softest, brownest eyes Lily had ever seen. Her pink tank top and blue shorts were a bit rumpled, but otherwise she seemed alright.

"I'm glad," Lily said, giving her an encouraging smile. She was comfortable with children, having raised four younger siblings. Well, three stepsiblings and a half-sibling, technically. It was adults, especially those of the opposite sex, who threw her for a loop.

"My name is Lily. What's yours?" she asked.

"Shanika," the little girl replied, her expression solemn.

"Do you live close by, Shanika?"

"Uh-huh." The girl nodded and pointed down the street at what looked like a two-story apartment building.

"Do your parents know where you are?"

"Uh-huh. Mama said quit makin' a ruckus'n' go play outside, an' I was hungry, so I went to get me some ice cream." Shanika smiled, warming up to Lily. She spoke with a strong southern twang, an accent Lily herself might have had but never developed due to her mother's strict emphasis on "proper English" when she was growing up.

"And what were you going to do after that?" Lily asked.

"I'm goin' to my friend's birthday party."

"Really? That sounds fun. But won't there be ice cream at the party?"

"Uh-huh. But I ain't at the party yet. Anyhow, it's hotter'n a goat's butt in a pepper patch. That's what mama allus says when she's wantin' some ice cream."

Lily laughed. "It is indeed hot. Why don't you let me and my friend Sebastian buy you another ice cream, since your last one got smushed?"

Shanika's eyes lit up and she nodded.

Lily took the girl's hand, ignoring Sebastian's confused look. Shrugging, he followed her as, hand in hand, Lily walked her new friend across the street to the 5 and Dime. Soon Shanika was holding a new cone piled high with dripping sweetness that she lapped up with glee.

"So how old is your friend turning today?" Lily asked casually as they all sat down on a bench outside the 5 and Dime.

"He gonna be ten."

"How long have you known him?"

"Oh, *foreva*," Shanika said, putting the kind of theatrical emphasis on the word that only a cute little girl with flopping braids could do. "Our school's real small, so we always inna same class."

"That's nice. So I bet you're really good friends, right?"

"Uh-huh. We allus play together. But today he was gettin' the party ready, so mama said I couldn't go 'til later."

"Well, do you think it's time to join the party?" Lily asked.

Finishing her last bite of ice cream, Shanika nodded.

"Would it be alright if we came along? We'd love to meet your friend. He sounds wonderful." Lily mentally crossed her fingers.

Shanika considered her request, face screwed up in thought. Then her expression cleared and she smiled brightly. "Okay! Will y'all stay an' play games with us?"

"Sure sweetie, we'd love to play. Why don't you show us how to get there?"

Shanika hopped off the bench and took Lily's hand, pulling her down the street while chatting animatedly about her favorite party games. Lily and Sebastian shared a knowing look over her head. The first part of the plan had worked. Lily only hoped the rest of it would go as smoothly.

★ ★ ★ ★

Their walk to Rob's house was, thankfully, uneventful, though Lily started noticing the now-familiar distorted flickers at the edge of her vision. Reality inside the loop was starting to act like the in-between space. Worried, she knew they couldn't afford to fail this time: there was no guarantee the magic would hold together for another loop.

They let Shanika ring the doorbell, which she did with enthusiasm. While they waited, Lily resisted the urge to glance behind her at the sheriff's cruiser parked across the street. The man had stared at them as they'd walked past, but there was no spark of recognition in his eyes. With all the parents bringing children to the party, she supposed he'd been told to look out for two adults alone, not someone accompanying a child.

She tensed when the doorknob turned, but to her surprise it was not Rob who opened it. It was a slender, sickly-looking boy who nonetheless had an excited light in his eyes and a festive party hat on his head.

"Hey, Shanika!"

"Hey, Bobby! I brought some friends with me. This here's Lily and that's Sebastian. They're real nice 'cause they saved me from this car that was gonna hit me! *And* they got me ice cream. Can they come to the party, too?"

"Sure," Bobby said, smiling up at them. "Thanks for helpin' Shanika. She's my best friend."

"We were happy to help," Lily said. "And it's nice to meet you, Bobby. Shanika was telling us all about what an amazing friend you are."

Bobby blushed and grinned lopsidedly.

"Come on, y'all," Shanika said, tugging on Lily and Sebastian's hands. "Let's go play."

Lily looked around nervously as Bobby led them through the house. Sooner or later, Rob would notice them and then they would find out if her little plan to infiltrate the household had worked. It wouldn't hurt to get on the kids' good side before then.

But the man of the house didn't appear, and soon they were outside, surrounded by shouting children about to play freeze tag. To Lily's surprise, Sebastian fell right in with them, egging them on and growling ferociously whenever he was "it." Noticing Bobby had trouble keeping up with the other children, he even joined forces with the boy and helped him dominate the game.

As for herself, she simply tried to keep up. Running was not a skill she needed or practiced in her duties as archives manager at Agnes Scott College.

Eventually, though, she got so involved she nearly jumped out of her skin when a hand grabbed her from behind, spinning her around to stare into Rob's livid face.

"Why, you little—" he began, but cut himself off and smoothed his face into a smile as his son trotted up. Sebastian, having spotted the fast-approaching confrontation, headed over as well.

"Hey, Pa," Bobby said. "Come play with us!"

"Uh…no, sorry son, not now. Me'n this gal here need to have us a chat."

"You mean Lily? Can't y'all talk later? We're playin' a game."

Rob's brow creased, and Lily could tell he was working on a kid-friendly version of what he was thinking. "Well, she ain't one of the guests, so I'm thinkin' she and her friend best skedaddle if they know what's good for 'em," he finally said.

"But, Pa, *I* know'em, and they're my friends! They helped Shanika and she knows 'em too, so they ain't strangers. Please, Pa, it's my birthday. Can't they stay?"

Lily held her breath as Rob's mouth formed a thin line. He looked back and forth between her, Sebastian, and his son's pleading expression. The moment stretched into uncomfortable silence, and she knew she had to do something.

Leaning in, she spoke quietly into Rob's ear, making one last attempt at reason, "I promise, we're not here to cause trouble, we just need to talk. You, Bobby, and everyone else here are in danger. Please, for the sake of your son, hear us out."

Rob exhaled sharply in annoyance but whispered back his assent. "Fine. But *after* the party. An' if ya'll cause a ruckus and ruin my boy's day, I'll whup ya both like a rented mule."

Forcing a smile back on his face, he released Lily's arm. "Alrighty, Bobby, they can stay. Now don't you play 'til the sun goes down. Food's nearabout ready."

"Sure, Pa! An' will you come play with us after that?"

Rob's smile turned genuine as he ruffled his son's hair. "If you ain't plumb tuckered out by then, Bobby boy. Now get on an' work up that appetite. I made mac 'n' cheese for y'all and I'm gonna need help eatin' it."

"Yeah!" Bobby cheered and pumped his fist, obviously in favor of the plan.

The children resumed playing with renewed vigor. They might have kept on forever if Lily hadn't convinced them to tackle Sebastian all at once, thus ending the game. Tired but happy, they all went inside for a birthday meal of epic proportions, topped off with cake and ice cream, much to

Shanika's delight. Afterwards the party progressed to presents and more games.

Through it all, Lily noticed the strange way Rob interacted with his son. He obviously loved the boy and took every opportunity to dote on him and be involved in the party. Yet his actions were exaggerated, and he tried too hard to stay busy. A few times when Bobby's attention was elsewhere, she caught him staring at his son with a sad and distant expression.

When the party was finally over, the guests began their trickling departure. Shanika gave them both a heartwarming hug before she left, assuring them she came to Bobby's house every day by herself so there was no need to walk her home.

Rob's attitude toward them hadn't changed over the course of the party. Now that the guests were gone, the air was thick with tension. Hoping to diffuse it, Lily offered to help clean up. After several surreptitious nudges to the ribs, Sebastian caught on and offered, too. Surprisingly, Rob accepted. They all got to work as Bobby gathered his new toys and carted them upstairs. Once everything was clean, Rob went up to make sure Bobby was settled and came back down carrying a small rectangular box.

Knowing what was in it, Lily felt her pulse quicken. But she refrained from saying anything and stepped on Sebastian's foot when he opened his mouth. They followed Rob to the kitchen table where he set the box down and motioned for them to have a seat.

"Alright. 'Afore I have a dyin' duck fit, tell me why I shouldn't throw y'all both outta my house. Or, better yet, lock y'all in the closet and let the sheriff learn you some manners."

Lily and Sebastian glanced at each other, and through silent agreement Lily spoke first.

"Look, Mr. Smith, let's stop pretending we don't all know what's going on here, alright?"

Rob stared hard at her for a long moment. Finally, he sighed and rubbed his face in frustration. "That'll be a mite bit hard, since I don't rightly know what's going on m'self. All I know is, every time I push a button on that contraption, I get another day with my boy, an' he gets another mighty fine birthday party."

Lily's brow crinkled. "Wait—so, if you don't know what it is, then how do you know how to use it?"

"I ain't got a cotton-pickin' clue! I found it in that antique shop aroundabout...well, I ain't rightly sure how long ago. I guess I lost count of the days. Anyhow, my boy loves history, an' he's always goin' on 'bout ancient civilizations and stuff he learned at school. This contraption reminded me of them funny calculators y'all see in textbooks, what are they called? With all them beads in a line?"

"An abacus?" Sebastian offered.

"Yeah, that's the one. I know, I know, it ain't the same shape, but it's got all them dials with funny scribbles on 'em. He's a sucker for collectin' doohickies like that. I even caught him diggin' out back once; dug a fair big hole 'afore I explained there ain't no Egyptians or Hittites or Greeks as ever lived here. He's a good kid, studies real hard. He just gets funny ideas in his head sometimes.

"I gave it to him this mornin'...well, a passel a mornings ago, I guess. When he picked it up, it sorta glowed for a sec. It ain't never done that when I touched it. I was fixin' to chuck it, but he gave me a look like a kicked pup so I let him keep it. He fiddled with it all mornin' 'til I made him put it away 'afore the party. That evenin' when I was cleanin'

I picked it up an' this piece popped out the end. I reckoned I'd broke the dern thing, so I tried to mash it back in. Things flashed around me real quick-like, and next I know it's mornin' again.

"I sure was glad Bobby sleeps in on Saturdays, 'cause I near as had me a conniption fit. But then I saw all his birthday stuff was wrapped up and all the food was back in the 'frigerator. I didn't have a doggone clue what to do, so I jus' acted normal. Bobby didn't remember a thing from the day 'afore an' the party went along jus' the same. No one said a thing 'bout it, so neither did I.

"That evenin', the second time 'round, I took it out and was jus' staring at it in my hands when the dern button popped out again, exactly the same as 'afore. I...well, I couldn't help m'self. It'd been a nigh on perfect day for Bobby, and I...I couldn't let it go. So I mashed it again."

"And here we are, days' worth of birthdays later," Sebastian said scathingly. "Do you realize you've trapped the whole town in this loop? You're keeping everyone here just to live your silly party over and over. That thing is a stolen family heirloom and a dangerous magical artifact. I'll thank you to give it back." He held out his hand.

Rob didn't react well to Sebastian's demand. He grabbed the box, pulling it protectively toward him as he glared across the table.

"That's hogwash. I bought it fair an' square."

Sebastian stood up. His tone was casual, almost joking, but his eyes glinted dangerously. "Regardless, sir, of how you acquired it, it's dangerous. You have no idea the fire you're playing with, so I highly recommend you hand it over."

That just made Rob's expression turn harder. He stood as well, opening his mouth to demand their immediate removal, no doubt. But Lily spoke first, voice stern.

"Mr. Smith, will you sit down, *please*. Sebastian, you too." When they hesitated, she gave them both her most withering glare. Rob caved first and sat down; Sebastian followed suit.

Turning to Rob, Lily spoke calmly but firmly. "Mr. Smith, it's imperative you understand what's going on before you make any rash decisions. As an archives manager, I have experience with these sorts of...artifacts. It may seem fantastical, but the device you have can indeed loop time. It creates a field of alternate reality and, as long as you continue resetting it, it repeats the time period set by its dials.

"The problem is its...energy source is running out. The field is breaking up and going haywire in some places, creating dangerous anomalies. This whole loop could disintegrate, and every man, woman, and child trapped here could cease to exist, get stuck in between realities, be turned inside out, or who knows what else. And it'll happen soon if you keep pushing that button. We need to break the spell, or better yet not reset the loop and let things return naturally to real time."

Rob stared at her, obviously trying to take it all in. "How'm I supposed to know if you're tellin' the truth and not jus' spinnin' a fancy yarn? An' if it's all that pow'ful, why would I give it over?"

Lily sighed, exasperated. "You'd know if you took a minute to actually look around and see what's happening. And you'll give it to me because you love your son too much to risk hurting him. Even if the loop wasn't in imminent danger of collapsing, this eternal repeat isn't healthy. No matter how enjoyable, one day can never be better than a lifetime. I know you want him to be happy, but keeping him from living his life isn't the way to do it."

She extended her hand, holding his gaze until his stubborn expression slowly crumbled. As it did, his shoulders slumped and his eyes filled with a weary despair that pierced Lily's heart to the core.

"I...I cain't give it to you. His mama passed a few years ago an' he's all I got left. This here's my last chance to be with him."

"What are you talking about?" asked Sebastian, alarmed. "He'll have other birthdays. What's so important about today?"

"No, he won't—" Rob's words came out as a choked sob. "He...he's got leukemia. The doctors s—say he won't last more'n s—six months. This here's the last birthday he'll ever have. I found a way to make him live longer, an' I cain't give it up. I won't!"

A stunned silence fell.

"Oh, Mr. Smith," Lily said, voice gentle and eyes burning with unexpected tears. "I'm...I'm so sorry."

"Yes, yes. It's all very touching and tragic, but it's entirely beside the point."

A refined voice spoke behind them, making them all jump. Lily turned to see a familiar, imposing figure standing in the archway between living room and kitchen. Heart sinking, she realized the door must have been left unlocked. The wizard's crisp suit was the exact same color gray as it had appeared to her in the antique store, though the rest of him now had color. His pale skin contrasted sharply with his raven black hair, and his eyes were a piercing blue, bluer even than Lily's own. He examined their stunned faces with an unconcerned air as he casually pointed a sleek and rather lethal-looking pistol in their direction.

"You!" Rob and Lily said at the same time.

"Yes, me, and I'm done playing games," the newcomer said. "This whole cloak-and-dagger business is incredibly tiresome. It's been hard enough navigating in and out of this damnable loop, but thanks to that imbecile's thick-headed stubbornness," he said, gesturing at Rob, "the loop is now so unstable that magic use is out of the question. I'm forced to resort to the crude barbarities of you mundanes."

Despite his apparent disgust toward the gun in his hand, his aim did not waver.

Looking at Rob, he continued. "That was quite a moving speech, Mr. Smith, but it doesn't invalidate what the young lady told you. Your son and everyone else here is in for an unpleasant end if you don't give me that artifact."

"You wouldn't..." Rob said, his nervousness and uncertainty evident as he eyed the gun. "You're bluffin'. Y'all are in this together!"

"We are most certainly not together," Sebastian interrupted, indignant. "That thing is mine. It's been in my family for years. If anyone gets it, it'll be me." He stood up and glared at the man in the archway, not in the least intimidated by the pistol. Lily hoped desperately he wouldn't do anything rash.

"So, you're a Blackwell, are you?" the wizard asked, eyebrow raised. "I'm sorry to break it to you, boy, but it's not yours. Your family stole it, and I'm here to take it back."

"Wha—?" Sebastian's mouth dropped open.

"Nobody's gonna take anythin'!" Rob said forcefully, standing up. "Y'all are gonna get outta my house, or I'll mash the button on this thing!" He waved the box containing the lugal-nam menacingly.

"Whoa, whoa!" Lily exclaimed, holding up her hands in a calming gesture as she, too, stood. "Just calm down, Mr. Smith. And whatever you do, *do not push that button.* The device's power is giving out and if you loop it again we could all die, including your son. Please, sit down and we'll discuss this like mature adults."

The man in the archway chuckled, though his tense body language belied his casual air as his eyes remained locked on Rob. "Yes, do take the young lady's advice, Mr. Smith. I would hate to have to hurt someone."

Lily eyed the wizard, her burning curiosity driving her to distraction despite the danger. She could feel him radiating power like a small sun. Usually wizards kept their power heavily masked, so as not to shine like a beacon to any magic user who wandered by. But this man hadn't the faintest hint of a mask, as if he were daring the world to take note. She also noticed he wasn't wearing the ward-ring she'd seen earlier. That implied he knew what would happen to anyone warded against the lugal-nam's magic when it reset. The in-between space was a dangerous place to be right now.

With considerable effort, she put aside the questions clamoring to be asked and focused back on Rob. "Look, I can't begin to imagine the pain you're going through. But that doesn't justify putting hundreds of lives in danger. What would your son say if he knew? And do you even know if Bobby wants to live the same day over and over? Have you asked him what he wants?"

"I know he don't wanna die," Rob said, voice choking up again. "Every day after his party, he says it was the best day in his life. Why wouldn't he wanna keep livin' it, 'stead'a dyin'?"

"But, Mr. Smith—"

"Jus' shut th' hell up!" he yelled, growing more upset. "I cain't let him die."

"Look, let's make this easy," the wizard interrupted. "I'll give you a hundred thousand dollars if you hand me the box. You can use the money for the best treatment possible. Maybe there's something the doctors can do."

Rob shook his head "No. There's nuttin' they can do. Leukemia's got no cure. This here's the only way."

"Hey," Sebastian said, shooting the wizard a nasty look before catching and holding Rob's gaze, expression full of a tender sadness Lily had never seen before. "We don't want your son to die, either, but we also don't want anyone else to get hurt. I know what kind of pain you're going through. I lost both my parents when I was a teenager. It was worse than dying, and it still hurts every day. I'd give anything, *anything,* to get them back. But I can't. Even if I used that device and prevented their deaths, it wouldn't fix things. They'd have still died in another life. I would have still spent years dealing with the pain. Even if I could get back a version of them in a different reality, our relationship would never be the same.

"Trying to keep your son alive by playing with time is hurting your relationship with him. You need to let him live the life he's been given and accept whatever comes after. He's accepted it, and you should, too. You have no right to decide his fate, and you could be endangering him even further. You can't change fate. You can't play God. Please, just give us the device and let him move on in peace." Sebastian held out his hand invitingly.

Rob looked torn, glancing between Sebastian and the gun in the wizard's hand.

"Enough of this tiring debate," the wizard said as he stepped forward. "Give me the box now or I'll—"

"You'll do what?" Sebastian asked, expression switching from tender to hard in an instant. The wizard froze, looking warily at the yellow-and-black police Taser that had suddenly materialized in Sebastian's other hand.

"Uh…Sebastian, what are you doing?" Lily asked, nervous that the wizard's aim had shifted to Sebastian's chest. "And where did you even get that thing?"

"Nicked it off the sheriff," Sebastian said absently, gaze still fixed on the wizard. "The guy was thicker than an oak tree. Didn't even notice. Not like you, Mr. Fancy Pants," he continued, addressing the wizard. "You seem to know what's going on, so I want answers. Who are you? How do you know my name? What do you mean, my family stole the lugal-nam?"

"Hmm, lugal-nam? So you *are* a wizard? Strange, you don't feel gifted. You, on the other hand, most definitely are." The wizard's gaze shifted to Lily and she felt a chill run down her spine at the hungry curiosity in his eyes.

"Hellooo," Sebastian said. "Over here. Let's stay focused, shall we? Just because I'm not a wizard doesn't mean I'm ignorant." He sounded sarcastic, but Lily could see worry in his face as he tried to draw the wizard's attention away from her.

With a "this isn't over" look at her, the wizard's eyes shifted back to Sebastian and a condescending smile slowly spread across his face. "That lugal-nam was passed down from generation to generation in my family for hundreds of years before one of your ancestors stole it, wanting all the power for himself, I'm sure. I've been searching for it for decades. You Blackwells are hard to pin down when you don't want to be found. I'll commend you on that. Now stop being a fool and put the Taser down."

Sebastian hesitated, putting his free hand in his pocket and half drawing it out with a look of disbelief. But then his expression hardened into one of resolve and he put both hands on the Taser, holding it steady. "No. Even if my ancestors did steal the lugal-nam, it was to keep it safe and out of the wrong hands. I'm thinking those wrong hands might include yours." Though his eyes were full of steel, Sebastian also quirked a smile, matching his opponent's mocking expression.

The wizard sighed. "Must we do this? Despite your forefather's thieving ways, I hold you no ill will. If you help me get the lugal-nam, you and your companion may depart unharmed. I'll even offer you ten thousand dollars to pay for your trouble."

"Ten thousand?" Sebastian asked, incredulous. "You offered the other guy a hundred."

"Yes, but you're not desperate. You don't have a dying son."

"Maybe not, but I do have dead parents."

"Indeed…yet you yourself said you can't change fate. Did all those pretty words mean nothing?"

Sebastian didn't reply. His smile had faded, but his gaze didn't waver. Lily could see the pain in his eyes and couldn't imagine the struggle he was going though. She waited, breathless, wanting to offer support but not daring to speak with both men on a hair trigger.

"What's going on?" A tremulous, child-like voice spoke from the stairs.

"Bobby, no!" Rob yelled, making a dash for his son.

Distracted by Rob, the wizard's attention faltered for a split second. Sebastian saw his chance and fired the Taser.

Chaos erupted.

The electrical shock made the wizard's hand clench, and a boom split the air as his gun fired. The slug hit Sebastian square in the chest and threw him backward.

"NO!" Lily's whole body went cold. Her ears were ringing so badly she couldn't even hear her own scream as she lunged for Sebastian's now prostrate form, bleeding out on the kitchen floor.

"No, no, no, no," she moaned, trying to press down on the bullet wound to stop the bleeding. All she achieved was hands stained red as the blood continued to seep out, soaking Sebastian's shirt. She looked around desperately, trying to force her shocked mind to come up with a plan. The wizard lay a few feet away, twitching, Taser probes still hanging off him. She noticed a slight waver in the air behind him, a flickering that jump-started her thought process.

Scrambling, she stumbled over Sebastian's limp form, heading for where Rob was clutching his son at the bottom of the stairs, eyes wide and staring in shock at the dying man on his floor. He'd dropped the box containing the lugal-nam in his dash for the stairs, and Lily scooped it up off the floor.

Opening it, she gazed upon the lugal-nam for the first time and was lost for a moment in wonder at its intricate beauty. Something about it drew her in, a sort of magical aura that radiated ancient power.

She shook herself. Everything depended on her getting this right. She only hoped the device had enough power left for what she needed to do.

Let it work, please let it work, she thought, refusing to consider the alternative.

Giving herself a few precious moments to carefully examine the dimmu runes, she turned one dial, then another, lining up the symbols in what she thought was the right combination. With a click the button on the end popped out as if eager to be pushed. Looking back at Sebastian's body, Lily was gripped by a moment of sheer panic. What if she'd read the runes wrong? What if the device didn't work?

It didn't matter. She couldn't sit there and watch her friend die. With a wordless prayer, she pushed the button.

Time shifted.

"...I'll even offer you ten thousand dollars to pay for your trouble."

There was a moment of silence in which the wizard looked expectantly at Sebastian. But Sebastian was staring at Lily. Unlike Rob and the wizard, he remembered what had just happened. With a nod of reassurance, she wordlessly asked him to trust her.

He gave a tiny nod and shifted his eyes back to the wizard. "Ten thousand?" he asked belatedly. "You offered the other guy a hundred."

The wizard's brow was knit in confusion at their silent exchange, but he continued anyway. "Yes, but you're not desperate. You don't have a dying son."

"Maybe not, but I do have dead parents," Sebastian replied, getting back into stride.

Ignoring the men's conversation, Lily took advantage of their focus on each other to shift slightly, looking behind the wizard and hoping what she'd seen before was still there.

It was.

With a lunge that would have made her long-ago high school gym coach proud, Lily tackled the wizard, pushing him violently backwards. Her push wasn't strong—she was no athlete—but it was enough to make him stumble back.

He had time for a startled cry, his reflexive movements setting off the gun, which put a bullet in the wall just above Sebastian's head. Then he was gone, fallen through the ripple in time behind him that led to who knew where.

Silence hung in the air, broken only by the ringing in Lily's ear. Her heart pounded like she'd just sprinted a mile and her limbs shook, adrenaline still rushing through her body.

"Wow...Lily..." Sebastian stammered, staring at her in shock and not a little awe.

Lily ignored him and faced Rob, not trusting her emotions enough yet to speak to the man she'd seen dying on the floor moments before. She suspected the vision of Sebastian's bleeding form would haunt her dreams for weeks. She'd examine that tangle of feelings later.

"Mr. Smith, now do you see how dangerous that device is? What it can drive men to do? For the love of your son, give it to us, and let us take it far away from here and leave you in peace."

"What's going on?" A tremulous, child-like voice spoke from the stairs leading to the second floor.

Rob looked over at the wide-eyed face of his son, expression tortured and eyes brimming with tears. He looked back at Lily, then at the spot in his living room where the wizard had stood. Finally, he nodded. Placing the box on the kitchen table, he went to his son.

"Nothing's goin' on, Bobby boy. Let's get you back in bed."

He ushered his son up the stairs, giving them one last, sad look over his shoulder.

Sebastian picked up the box and looked at Lily, uncertainty in his eyes.

"It's your family's heirloom, your family's burden," she said, understanding his unspoken struggle. "It's up to you."

She saw the pain from years of loneliness and loss flash across his features. Then he looked away, expression unreadable. Opening the box, he took out the lugal-nam and gazed at it briefly. Lily could only guess what wild hopes and desires were running through his mind.

Then in one swift motion he raised it above his head and threw it violently down on the bare kitchen floor.

The artifact's fragile clay form shattered and everything around her vanished into blackness.

Lily woke to find herself lying half on and half off of a concrete sidewalk. Her head, shoulder, and hip throbbed painfully. She sat up, holding her head with one hand to try to relieve the splitting headache that was fast developing. With a jolt of relief, she spotted Sebastian several feet away, also draped halfway across the curb. He looked to have as bad a headache as she, but was no worse for wear.

Looking around she saw other people as well. All were in various states of picking themselves up off the ground. Several cars sat at crazy angles in the road as if their drivers had momentarily lost control, then screeched to a halt. Thankfully, no one appeared to be hurt.

Realizing they were finally back in real time, Lily scrabbled at her back jeans pocket, pulling out her phone and turning it on. It was 5:25 PM, Thursday, July 5. She'd entered the loop at 5:25 PM on Saturday evening, June 30. Her heart sank. They would be frantic at the library. Penny, her assistant, always stressed out whenever Lily took a day off. For her to be gone four whole days with no notice…oh, boy.

"Um, Sebastian," she said.

She heard a grunt, a groan, and then, "Yeah?"

"Next time you need help finding a time looping device and saving a whole town from certain death and destruction…don't call me, okay?"

"…got it. No calling you when the world needs saving and you're the only one who can help."

"Oh, shut up."

"Yessir, ma'am."

Epilogue

THEY LEFT SEBASTIAN'S CAR IN PITTS. HE'D BEEN STUCK THERE A week longer than Lily, and he had that much more sleep to catch up on. He conked out as soon as he dropped into her passenger seat.

They didn't stick around to explain to the confused population of Pitts what had happened. Magic on that scale affecting a large portion of the uninformed public hadn't happened in a long time. Lily felt it was wisest to make herself scarce. Hopefully no one would remember them, or else everyone would write the whole experience off as a strange dream. A strange dream lasting several weeks. If he were smart, Rob would sweep up the fragments of that artifact, bury them somewhere remote, and claim he knew nothing. She regretted missing the chance to study such an ancient and powerful device. But perhaps it was for the best.

She'd also hoped to talk to Rob about their family tree. There had to be magical blood in there somewhere for Bobby to have turned on the lugal-nam. But perhaps that was also a path best left untrod. She didn't think Rob would appreciate that sort of life-changing news, considering his son's days were numbered. Not even magic could cure terminal illness.

Though she didn't feel much better than Sebastian looked, multiple energy drinks and a mind racing with questions kept her awake for the few hours it took to drive back to Atlanta, deposit Sebastian at his apartment, then drive home and drag herself up to her own apartment.

She briefly considered calling someone at the college to let them know she was back, but she couldn't bring herself to deal with the drama just then. Groaning inside and knowing there would be hell to pay in the morning, she unlocked her front door and made it as far as the couch before passing out, while an anxious Sir Kipling purred and rubbed on her leg dangling over the edge.

The next morning she called the library and tried to explain that she'd had to go home unexpectedly for a family emergency and hadn't had a chance to call until now. Her boss, the director of library services, calmly accepted her lame excuse and said she was glad Lily was home safe. She suggested Lily take the day off and come in to work on Monday.

Thirty minutes later, two cops showed up at her door.

She spent a good hour answering their questions, trying to make her story as bland and uninteresting as possible. She could tell they weren't buying it. But it had only been a missing persons report, after all. And since she was, quite obviously, no longer missing, there wasn't much more for them to do but wish her a restful weekend and go on their way.

Later that day she went by to check on Sebastian. She found his door unlocked and him, fully clothed, fast asleep on his bed. Apparently no one had missed him enough to file a missing persons report. She went out and got him some groceries—it was the least she could do—and when she got back he was awake.

They ate a silent, sober meal together.

Finally, she couldn't keep quiet any longer. "Sebastian, why did you break it? I mean, it got us out of the loop, but if we'd have waited a bit longer the loop would have ended anyway."

He was silent a long time before answering.

"I figured if I broke it, that would keep Mr. Fancy Pants from popping back in on us. I didn't like that guy one bit." He glared into the bowl of tomato soup she'd made for him.

"Is that all?" she prompted after another long pause.

"No...I meant what I said about not playing God. But if I'd kept the lugal-nam, knowing what it does, I'd have tried to bring them back and damn the consequences."

Lily let the conversation drop, not needing to ask who "they" were. She wondered what she would have done in his situation. Well, she was, in a way. To what lengths would she go to find her father? What difficult decisions might she have to make, and what consequences would they have? Looming above those questions was the memory of a frightening, dangerous, yet annoyingly familiar wizard she'd pushed into a time-rift with her own hands. She wondered if he'd found his way back to real time yet. She also wondered who he was and how he might be connected to her family. Most of all, she wondered when and where she might meet him again.

A week later, more visitors arrived. She answered the firm knock to find two black-suited agents on her doorstep, a man and a woman. She was immediately struck by how handsome the man looked, and the unexpected ambush of her mind by such embarrassing thoughts left her flustered and searching for an appropriate greeting.

The man, sensing her hesitation, spoke first as he held up a badge for her to see. "Good afternoon, Miss Singer. My name is Agent Grant and this is Agent Meyer. We're with the FBI. We'd like to ask you a few questions about an incident in Pitts. Do you mind if we come in?"

Great, she thought. Just great.

Glossary

Agnes Scott College - a private liberal arts college in downtown Decatur, Georgia, located within metro Atlanta. Founded in 1889, the name was changed in 1890 to Agnes Scott Institute to honor the mother of the college's primary benefactor, Col. George Washington Scott. Though originally offering classes to elementary age and up, by 1906 the name was changed again to Agnes Scott College and remains today a women's-only college.

aluminum - a metal favored by wizards for its usefulness in absorbing large amounts of magic because of its high energy density potential. Safer and more stable than lithium, it is widely used in crafting spell anchors (see dimmu runes) either as a raw material or an inlay. While spells can be cast onto any substance but wrought iron, aluminum better absorbs the magic fueling the spell, thus making the spell more potent and long-lasting (as long as it is cast in conjunction with the proper dimmu runes and sealing spells).

Basement, the - the magical archive beneath the McCain Library containing a private collection of occult books on magic, wizardry, and arcane science, as well as an assortment of artifacts and enchanted items. Created in 1936 during the library's original construction, it is accessed through a secret portal in the broom closet of the library's own basement archive. At any point in time, the Basement has a gatekeeper, the wizard tasked with its maintenance and protection and upon whom rests the control of its magic. This collection of knowledge was bequeathed as a public resource to wizardkind, but, because of the decline of wizards in modern society, has been very little used by anyone but its gatekeeper. Lily Singer is the current gatekeeper, with Madam Barrington as her predecessor.

coprolalia - the involuntary and repetitive use of obscene language, as a symptom of mental illness or organic brain disease. Often confused with Tourette's syndrome, which actually covers a wide spectrum of tic disorders.

crafting - the art of creating and enchanting objects. Such objects, once made, can exist and operate separately from their creator or even magic in general, as the controlling spells are anchored to dimmu runes carved, inlaid, or otherwise affixed to them. To craft properly, you must not only know the properties of your materials, but also the dimmu runes needed to attain the desired result.

dimmu - [dim + mu = {dim = to make, fashion, create, build (du = to build, make + im = clay, mud)} + {mu = word, name, line on a tablet}] the Enkinim word for runes of power, the script used to write Enkinim, the language of power. In and of itself, this script is not magical, and a mundane could write it all day without achieving anything. Dimmu runes are used by wizards to anchor their spells. Infused with magic from the Source, these runes enable and guide the carrying out of the desired enchantment and can preserve the enchantment's effect long after the spell is cast.

eduba - [e + dub + a = {e = house, temple, plot of land} + {dub = clay (tablet), document} + {a = genitive marker}] the Enkinim word for library, used by ancient Sumerians to indicate the houses where their clay writing tablets were kept. To a wizard, however, it describes a book containing their personal archive of knowledge. Similar to the mundane notion of grimoires, edubas are full of much more than simply spells. They accumulate centuries of history, research, and personal notes as they are passed down, usually from parent to child or teacher to student within powerful wizard families. The knowledge in them is magically archived, such that you must summon the desired text to the physical pages before it can be read. This allows for vast stores of information to be carried around in one physical book.

elwa - fae word of greeting. It carries deeper meaning, however, than a simple hello. It is a request to commune with or share the presence of the named fae. The request may be denied or ignored, in which case the supplicant must withdraw. It is considered extremely rude to ask a second time.

Enkinim - [Enki + inim = {Enki = Sumerian god of creation and friend of mankind} + {inim = word; statement; command, order, decree}) words of power, the language of magic by which wizards control and direct the Source. Named after the Sumerian god Enki, who, it was said, taught mankind language, reading, and writing.

fae - one of the three species of magic users (human, fae, and angel/demon). Myth says they were created to help steward the earth, and that long ago they worked side-by-side with man to nurture it. But they have long since faded from sight and memory, and very little reliable record remains about them (though theories abound).

fae glamour - a type of fae magic by which fae disguise their true shape. They also use it to create illusions or temporarily change the appearance of inanimate objects.

While wizards can cast their own type of glamour to achieve a similar effect, their scrying spells can not see through fae glamour. It can be defeated using a seeing stone, something only fae can make. A fae can see through another fae's glamour.

ga-arhus-a ken - Enkinim meaning "it is forgiven," a phrase used by Lily to unmake a curse that was cast to dispel only once the offended has forgiven the offender.

Gilgamesh - figure from ancient Sumerian lore. Opinions differ on whether or not he was historical. Possibly also mentioned in Biblical text by the name of Nimrod. In wizard legend it is said he was the original recipient of magic from the gods, and all wizards are his blood descendants. Considered the most powerful wizard in all of history—almost a god—he searched for, but never found, the source of immortality.

Grimoli'un - a mold fae befriended by Sebastian Blackwell, who calls him Grimmold. The *'un* of the name denotes masculine character. Grimmold has a sense of smell so good he can track things across dimensions. He has a weakness for specially aged pizza (Sebastian's usual bribe in exchange for Grimmold's services) and is very allergic to soap or cleaning fluids of any kind.

human - one of the three species of magic users (human, fae, and angel/demon), and the only one of the three with a direct connection to the Source. Whereas fae and angels/demons were created with a set amount of magical power proportional to their status, humans have no innate limit. They are limited only by their own will, discipline, and skill, as well as the frailty of their mortal bodies. Also, not all humans can use magic. While all fae and angels/demons are innately magical, only certain humans descended from the wizard lines manifest the ability to access the Source and manipulate magic. It is thought the difference is genetic and inherited, but no one yet knows how or why.

in-between, the - a dangerous place of nonexistence between realities where one is held separate from the flow of time. A person could become stuck there if they were in a time loop and it was reset but failed to take them with it. Such a thing could happen if they were wearing a particularly sensitive ward preventing active magic from influencing them, thus preventing the looping magic from returning them to the proper place and time.

initiate - a term traditionally used to indicate a member of a wizard family who is not a wizard. Because not all children born to wizards or wizard-mundane couples could use magic—yet were still raised within the magical community with knowledge of its secrets—there arose the need for a distinguishing word for someone not magical, yet not ignorant like a mundane. Because these mundane children of wizards often became the butlers, valets, housekeepers, etc., of wizards, the term initiate has come to mean someone who works for a wizard family, caring for them and keeping their secrets. It is an old-fashioned term, generally used by the very traditional. Most modern wizards simply call all non-magic humans mundanes, whether they know about magic or not. With the decline of wizard families and magic use in general, along with society's general acceptance of, rather than fear of, magic, the existence of initiates in the traditional sense has all but disappeared.

Jackson mansion, the - a mansion built in the southern plantation house style by Paul Jackson in the mid-1800s.

Located in southwestern Georgia on the Chattahoochee river, it fell into disuse and disrepair because of a curse cast on it in 1909 by Annabelle Witherspoon, the jilted lover of Francis Jackson (Paul's son). After an early death, Francis's ghost remained behind and haunted the house until the curse was unmade by Lily Singer approximately a hundred years later.

Jastiri'un - an elemental fae befriended by Sebastian Blackwell, who calls him Jas. The *'un* of the name denotes masculine character. Jas can control light and sound (mechanical and electromagnetic waves). Like most pixies, he has a weakness for alcohol, which Sebastian often trades him for various services.

lugal-nam - [lugal + nam = {lugal = king; master (lu = man + gal = big)} + {nam = planning ability; destiny}] literally translated *master of destiny*, it is the name given to a device created long ago by powerful wizards that can loop time by creating alternate timelines that repeat until the magic ends, at which point they rejoin "real" time. Made of clay and about six inches long by an inch and a half wide, it looks like a cylinder made up of rotating dials.

McCain Library - the library of Agnes Scott College, a private liberal arts women's college near downtown Atlanta. Built in 1936 to replace the smaller Andrew Carnegie Library constructed in 1910, it was originally still called the Carnegie Library, then later renamed the McCain Library after the college's second president in 1951. Complete with four main floors, a grand reading room, and three attached floors dedicated to the stacks, this building is Lily Singer's workplace and domain. She is the college's archives manager, and her office is located on the library's main floor. The basement floor contains the library's archives as well as the portal to the secret magical archive of which Lily is the gatekeeper.

Möbius strip - a surface with only one side and only one boundary. For example, if you take a strip of paper and give it a half-twist, then join the ends together to form a loop, you have made a Möbius strip. If you took a pencil and drew a line along the strip, you would return to where you'd started, having drawn a line on both sides without ever leaving the paper or crossing an edge.

mundane - a term used by wizards to denote non-magical humans. Generally, mundanes are ignorant of the existence of magic, the notable exception being witches. Other enlightened mundanes include members of wizard families who were born without the ability to use magic. These non-magical members of the wizard community were traditionally known as initiates. Historically, the term mundane was derogatory and insulting. Accusing a wizard or initiate of being "mundane" was paramount to calling them ignorant fools. The wizard community looked down on mundanes and considered them little more than animals. The fact that mundanes regularly executed anyone they suspected of using magic helped to solidify wizards' negative attitude toward them. That attitude has largely disappeared with the advance of society, though there still exists a lingering feeling of superiority among wizards.

Pilanti'ara - a plant fae befriended by Sebastian Blackwell, who calls her Pip. The *'ara* of the name denotes feminine character. As a plant fae, Pip has a certain area she is responsible for. Within that area she cares for all growing things. Like most pixies, she has a weakness for alcohol, which Sebastian often trades her for various services.

Pitts - a tiny town in south central Georgia. It is the location of Lily Singer and Sebastian Blackwell's fated adventure with the lugal-nam, a time-looping device that trapped them in Pitts until they could find it and save everyone from the time loop.

pixie - any fae that are small, quick, and flighty. This is purely a human term and has no relation to actual fae taxonomy (naming and classification). However, it is true that most pixies are energetic, fun-loving, and have a weakness for alcohol, which they can metabolize in vast amounts compared to their body mass without getting drunk. Of all the fae, they are the ones most familiar to, and seen by, humans because of their curiosity and lack of fear.

power anchor - a crafted object—usually something small and wearable like an amulet, necklace, or ring—that wizards use to focus and amplify their magic so as to cast more precise and powerful spells. For particularly powerful spells, wizards can create a one-time-use, secondary power anchor which they might draw or carve on the floor to further channel their magic.

runes of power - also known as dimmu runes, these are the symbols used to write Enkinim, the language of power that shapes magic. They are similar in appearance to the cuneiform script used in Mesopotamia during ancient times.

seeing stone - traditionally a triangular stone with a hole through it, though the stone can be any shape and still work. In ancient times these stones were made by the fae and given to certain humans so they could look through the hole and see past fae glamour. Few were preserved and passed down and so are rare today, for the fae have long since withdrawn from regular contact with humankind and give no more such gifts as they did in times past.

Source, the - the place from which all magic comes. While many creatures and parts of nature are innately magical, filled with the Source's power, wizards are the only beings in the universe born with an innate connection to it and the ability to draw on it at will. The Source is not sentient, only raw power. Magic drawn from the Source has to be shaped and directed by the caster's will using words of power (Enkinim). Incorrect use of Enkinim or poor control over a spell can cause backfires or spell mutations, resulting in a different outcome than intended and sometimes causing the injury or death of the caster. Though many known, reliable spells exist, the power of the Source is, in theory, limited only by the willpower and knowledge of the caster. Though safe to use within limits and with the proper training, many wizards over the years have died from overestimating their own strength or attempting dangerous spells which they did not properly understand. Thus, use of magic by modern wizards is in decline. With the rise of mundane technology, many wizards feel magic use is not worth the trouble or cost.

spell circle - a simple line or mark on the ground providing a visual aid and anchor to the casting of any sort of circle, such as a shield circle or circle of containment. Spell circles can be permanently engraved or carved into a surface accompanied by dimmu runes that add to the stability and effectiveness of whatever casting is being done.

spell of: containment - a kind of spell circle used to contain magic. It is usually cast as a safety measure when doing spell work.

spell of: shielding - a kind of spell used to shield the caster from magic. One type—a barrier through which magic cannot enter—is often cast as a spell circle. Another type—a selective spell that blocks only incoming active or targeted magic—is commonly used in personal wards.

spell of: text transference - a spell by which a wizard can copy text from one book to another. Particularly useful in archiving information into an eduba.

truth coin - a silver coin given to Sebastian Blackwell by his father. It is inscribed with dimmu runes and enchanted to grow warm in the presence of lies. The degree of warmth is directly proportional to the degree of the lie.

ward - magical protection of some kind, usually cast into an anchor such as a bracelet (personal ward) or into runes set in/around a location (stationary ward). Ward spells can be customized to do a variety of things. Personal wards usually contain a combination of a shield spell along with various minor spells that help protect the bearer from weariness, sickness, or other physical harm. Stationary wards put up around a house or created to protect a certain location or object, can be set to protect against specific things (just wizards, or alternately, just mundanes, for example). They can also be customized to prevent the passage of physical objects, sound, light, etc.

witch - a mundane who, through trades, favors, and alliances with other beings, gains magical power or the service of said beings. "Something given, something gained," is the way of a witch. While uncommon, the other two magical species (fae and angels/demons) have been known to form alliances with humans, mundane and wizard alike. Besides directly gaining other beings' magic, witches also often trade for the services of various supernatural beings. Many witches favor demonic pacts, as demons are the most eager for contact with humans. Such pacts, however, usually end badly for the witch, or else the witch is irrevocably changed, sometimes tricked or forced into subjugation to whatever demon they were trying to control. Spirits in their various forms are one of the other more common partners of witches. But since they are incorporeal and have no need for physical things, they can be hard to bargain with and, by nature, are unstable. Fae, while shy of humans and largely unknown to them, do occasionally form pacts. Historically, witches who allied with the fae were known as druids, but the term has largely fallen out of use because they are now so rare.

wizard - a human with the ability to access the Source and manipulate its power. The ability is thought to be genetic, as it seems to be passed from parent to child. Legend says magic was given to Gilgamesh and so only his descendants inherited it. Like most inherited genes, it can be diluted by mixing with normal human genes. So a wizard marrying a mundane is less likely to produce wizard children than a wizard-wizard union, though even those are not guaranteed to have all wizard children. A wizard's abilities are not instinctive, they are a skill that must be taught and mastered to use effectively.

words of power - the language (Enkinim) used by wizards to control their magical power. Passed down over the centuries, these words help shape and direct a wizard's spells, both activating and limiting their effects. Though many set spells exist, new ones can be discovered and old ones customized. The stronger a wizard's will, the more adroit their mind, and the better their understanding of Enkinim, the more they can do with magic. Magical experimentation can, however, be extremely dangerous.

Turn the page
for a preview of Lydia Sherrer's
second Lily Singer Adventures book

LOVE, LIES, AND HOCUS POCUS: REVELATIONS

Now in paperback and ebook

Chapter 1

Unexpected Conversations

Beams of late afternoon sunlight poured through Lily Singer's living room window, casting a bright patch of warmth on the rug. It was the only bit of July heat that made it into the air-conditioned refuge of her apartment. She sat cross-legged in the bright rectangle surrounded by open books and scattered papers. Her cat, Sir Edgar Allan Kipling, lay artfully sprawled across the mess, paws in the air and fluffy tummy soaking up the warmth like a sponge. Being a cat, he always seemed to be lying on the exact paper she was looking for, no matter where she moved him.

Lily usually did her research and casting in the Basement, her magical archive beneath the McCain Library of Agnes Scott College, where she worked as archives manager. Yet, the Basement lacked natural light, so she'd relocated to her living room in an attempt to translate the cuneiform from a fragment of clay tablet the size of a matchbox. Its worn marks were exceptionally hard to see, so the sunshine helped.

Thus far, by cross-referencing her most reliable lexicon with archaeological accounts dating to the nineteenth century, she'd been able to confidently identify only a single grouping of marks. They made reference to Ninmah, the Sumerian goddess of the earth and animals. More fascinating than the cuneiform, however, were the *dimmu* runes hidden beneath, invisible to the mundane, non-wizard eye. They were easier to see but no less confusing, as they differed from the standardized runes in her *eduba*—her personal archive contained within a single, enchanted tome. She assumed the runes differed because they predated the centuries of study and research she benefited from. Whatever they meant, exactly, the runes appeared to be part of a controlling spell. Without the complete tablet for context, however, she couldn't know for sure.

Technically, she was supposed to be working on the engravings for her new ward bracelet. Madam Barrington, her teacher in the wizarding arts as well as the former Agnes Scott archives manager, had lent her a standard ward after her original bracelet broke under the strain of magical backlash. It was enough to tide her over, but it was no replacement for a true, personally crafted ward. While digging through the Basement's drawers looking for supplies, however, she'd come across this fragment. *Enkinim*, the language of magic and therefore her primary study, was related to Sumerian in the same way magical dimmu runes were related to cuneiform. Curiosity and the promise of a challenge had been too much to resist.

She was peering at the fragment when a ringing interrupted her. Laying the piece of clay down on a pile of reference papers, she headed for her purse in the bedroom. As an introvert, she had few friends, and maintained an observant, rather than interactive, presence online, and so rarely kept her phone nearby. Glancing at the caller ID, she was surprised but delighted to see who it was. Madam Barrington didn't often use the phone.

"Good evening, Ms. B."

"Good evening, Miss Singer," she replied. Despite having been Lily's mentor for the past seven years, Madam Barrington was old-fashioned to the core and rarely addressed anyone by their first name. "I trust I'm not interrupting anything important?"

"Nothing that can't wait. To what do I owe the pleasure?"

"If you are able to excuse yourself from holding office hours tomorrow, an opportunity to further your professional and magical knowledge has arisen. The Tablet of Eridu exhibit at the Clay Museum will be closing at the end of the month. The artifact is on loan from the Hermann Hilprecht Museum of the University of Pennsylvania and has great historical as well as magical significance. I worked in partnership with the Clay Museum's curator two years ago when the exhibit opened; they have requested my help again to ensure the artifact's safe return. I agreed on the condition that you be allowed to assist. I am, after all, retired." Lily heard the faintest hint of dry humor in her mentor's voice and smiled. Like all wizards, Madam Barrington was long-lived and well preserved. She'd retired to let Lily take over management of the archives, not because of age or infirmity.

"I'd be delighted to join you. Fall term is a good month away and the summer students rarely darken my door. When and where shall I meet you?"

"Nine o'clock tomorrow morning at the Clay Museum. It is located on Emory University grounds."

"I'll be there," Lily said, making a note in her datebook.

"Very good, Miss Singer. I shall see you then."

They exchanged farewells and Lily hung up, thoughtful. She was familiar with Emory. It was a private research university north of Agnes Scott in the Druid Hills area of Atlanta. She'd been to their archives once or twice, as well as taken a few of their library science classes to augment her work experience at McCain Library, but she had never visited the Clay Museum.

Returning to her patch of sunlight and pile of papers, she was horrified to find Sir Kipling licking the clay fragment.

"Stop that! Shoo, shoo!" Lily hurried over and Sir Kipling, knowing he was in trouble, fled to relative safety underneath her desk.

"You ridiculous cat. Why must you bother everything?" she lamented to herself, picking up the fragment. Examining it, she was relieved to see it was barely damp at all, with no damage to its markings. A glance under the desk revealed her errant pet, who was now cleaning his paw with supreme unconcern, pausing occasionally to blink at her.

"Cats," she grumbled, settling back down in the patch of sunlight. She needed to get more deciphering done before the daylight weakened and she had to start thinking about bed. Nine a.m. came early, and she wanted to look, and feel, her best for an appointment at a prestigious university museum.

Lily woke Wednesday morning, not to the sound of her alarm clock, but to the soothing vibrations of a purring cat. She had an uncomfortable feeling she'd overslept but was distracted from it by the warm, heavy ball of fur settled comfortably on her chest.

Groaning, she tried to push him off. "Kip, you better not have turned off my alarm again."

Sir Kipling, however, didn't want to move. He dug his claws into the sheets and resisted her groggy attempt to dislodge him. "Well, if it weren't so loud and annoying, I wouldn't have to take matters into my own paws," he protested.

"It's *supposed* to be loud and annoying to wake me—"

She froze, going cross-eyed in an attempt to see the feline perched atop her. Her muddled, half-asleep brain tried, and failed, to make sense of what she'd just heard. It had sounded like meowing, but also like words. She stared at her cat and he stared back, eyes half-lidded.

"Did you…?" She paused, giving her head a shake to dislodge the cobwebs in her brain. "I thought I heard…good grief, I'm imagining a conversation with my cat. I need a hot shower." She sat up for real this time, her movement threatening to spill Sir Kipling onto the bedcovers.

Twisting with cat-like agility, he launched off her chest and landed on the edge of the bed in a dignity-preserving move, then turned to lick his mussed fur into submission. "A hot shower won't fix your problems," he commented between licks.

Lily stared, speechless, no longer sure of her own sanity.

Sir Kipling paused his ministrations to look at her. "If you insist on sitting there being shocked, you might as well make yourself useful and pet me."

"I—" She stopped, then tried again. "You…talk?"

A smug look was all the reply she got.

"Wait, that's not—since when?" Lily was still shocked, but her brain at least had started working again. She'd adopted Sir Kipling as a stray kitten during her last year of college and had never gotten the slightest inkling he was anything but a normal cat.

"Since now," he stated matter-of-factly.

"Don't be silly. Cats don't randomly start—" she paused, suddenly suspicious. "Was it that fragment of tablet? Wonderful. Just splendid. What did you do?"

He sniffed archly. "You'd think you weren't happy to talk to me. Well, good morning to you, too. I'm just fine, thanks for asking."

Lily rolled her eyes. He was perfectly healthy but probably wouldn't cooperate unless she mollified him. Typical cat.

"I trust you're well this morning? Did whatever you got up to last night damage anything vital?" She couldn't resist a bit of sarcasm, but he ignored it.

"Now that you mention it, there *is* this place on my back that's been itching all night—"

"Sir Edgar Allan Kipling," she interrupted in a voice that brooked no nonsense. "To the point, please."

"Well, if you insist," he said, taking his time to stretch and yawn before continuing. "I did nothing at all. I was just minding my own business when that piece of dirt you've been staring at—"

"You mean the clay fragment?"

Sir Kipling stopped, ears tilted back in annoyance. Lily closed her mouth. After a deliberate pause, he continued. "Yes, the piece of dirt. It started glowing and then…well, let's just say interesting times are coming, and someone thought you could use a little help."

"What? What's that supposed to mean? What's coming? Who are you talking about?"

"Well, I *could* answer your questions, but then you'd be late for your meeting."

Glancing at her alarm clock, she yelped and jumped out of bed, heading for the shower. She had barely thirty minutes to do what normally took an hour, and she would have to skip breakfast.

Hand on the bathroom door, she turned and glared at her cat, who had settled comfortably onto the warm spot she'd just vacated. His eyes had closed, as if in sleep, and all four paws were tucked under him, making him look like a fluffy loaf of bread—a catloaf.

"This isn't over, Sir. You and I will be having a very long conversation when I get home."

She didn't wait for his reply as she rushed into the bathroom to get ready.

Thanks so much for reading this book. If you enjoyed the story and want to see more such tales published, please take a brief moment to post a review. Book reviews help improve authors' sales and ranking and so are a great way to show support to your favorite author.

If you'd like to stay up to date on Lydia Sherrer's newest publications, go to lydiasherrer.com/subscribe to sign up for her email newsletter. This is where you can receive behind-the-scene sneak peeks of stories, book giveaways, and chances to get involved in the story-making process.

Lydia would love to connect with you online. Take a moment to check out the links below.

Read all about Lydia Sherrer and her books at lydiasherrer.com

Like on Facebook facebook.com/lydiasherrerauthor

Follow on Twitter twitter.com/lydiasherrer

About the Author

Lydia Sherrer is an author whose goal is to leave the world a better place than she found it. Growing up in rural Kentucky, she was thoroughly corrupted by a deep love for its particular brand of rolling countryside, despite the mosquitoes and hay fever. She was instilled with a craving for literature early on, and her parents had to wrestle books away from her at the dinner table. Though she graduated with a dual BA in Chinese and Arabic, having traveled the world, she came home and decided to stay there. She currently resides in Louisville, KY, with her loving and supportive husband and their very vocal cat.

Made in the USA
Middletown, DE
14 December 2017